I'm Not Holding The Coats!

Jill Rodgers

This is a work of fiction. Any names or characters, businesses or places, events or incidents, are fictitious. Any resemblance to actual persons, living or dead, or actual events is purely coincidental.

Copyright © 2023 Jill Rodgers

All rights reserved.
No part of this book may be reproduced or used in any manner without the prior written permission of the copyright owner, except for the use of brief quotations in a book review.

All content and images are property of Jill Rodgers, Stories from the Lodge.

Reprinted only by permission.

ISBN 9798852740199
First paperback edition April 2023.

Cover and Formatting by Rachel Weber
Layout by Rachel Weber

Printed by Printer Amazon KDP

Stories From The Lodge
storiesfromthelodge.2021@gmail.com

Dedication

*I would never have started this novel, much less finished it, without the
encouragement of the Riccall Writer's Group. Your individual talents are an
inspiration, your friendship invaluable.
Like Lizzie, I had begun to think life's opportunities had passed me by. You
gave me the courage and confidence to try something new. You did it with
constructive criticism and great humour.
Long may we continue to meet, talk, laugh and write.
Thank you all.*

Chapter 1

It started with a comment from my friend Sandra.

"Honestly," she said as she put the tray of drinks down on our table, "once a woman gets to sixty she becomes invisible!"

We were in the pub for our usual Friday lunch. There are four of us who go there most weeks, after our Over 60's exercise class at the local leisure centre. We jump about and stretch in varying degrees of enthusiasm, telling ourselves we are keeping fit and burning up calories, then go to have a meal of almost pure carbohydrate to make up for it.

Every week we talk about putting the app on our phones so that we can order our meals from our seats, like it says on the little label thing on the table. They make it sound so easy that we did try once, but after we thoroughly confused each other we gave up and decided we would do what we always do; take it in turns to go to the bar with a list. We can't remember four drinks and four mains at our age.

So it was Sandra's turn this week and when she came back after waiting ages to be served, she was spitting feathers.

"There must have been six people served before me who had all come to the bar after me! It's like you don't exist!"

We all made tutting, sympathetic noises as we sorted out my diet coke from Pat's full strength one, then gave Sandra her G and T and Trudy her red wine.

"I know just what you mean," I said. "Even if you're talking to someone, it's like they can't wait to get rid of you. I was in the mobile phone shop for ages yesterday, setting up a new contract. I could tell the girl was really hoping she could finish with me quickly because I only wanted a basic phone and a cheap deal. She was looking at the next person in the queue and rolling her eyes at him, because she needed to explain things to me more than once."

"Yes," agreed Pat, "even in the charity shop, where most of us volunteers are getting on a bit, the customers get impatient if we can't remember how the till works. I hate having to call the manager down from the office upstairs, but it's so much more complicated than the old tills I used when I was working, years ago."

Trudy nodded in agreement but she doesn't seem to have the same problems as the rest of us. She is by far the youngest of the four of us anyway, but she keeps herself young and trendy. I have heard her described unkindly as mutton dressed as lamb, but that was by someone whose husband she was flirting with at the time. The rest of us envy her youthful looks, but accept that she looks great for her age.

I nodded sadly. "I know we all feel the same, but I wonder in my case if it's partly my fault. Life seems to have passed me by. If I had my time again, I would definitely be a bit more pushy, take more chances. When the children were growing up we gave them lots of opportunities to try exciting activities, go-karting, sailing, rock climbing. I was always so self conscious, I left it to John to do stuff with them. In the end they stopped asking me. I always sat at the side and held everybody's coats, even when they were just swimming in the sea on holiday. I think I was invisible even in those days."

Trudy leaned over and patted my hand.

"Hey, life is not over yet, honey," she said. "Take any chances that come up."

It was later in the day that this conversation came back to me, when I woke up from an afternoon nap to find I had missed the first half of Pointless. I suddenly realised it didn't matter. In fact, nothing I did really mattered any more, it was all pretty pointless.

Don't get me wrong, I was not getting maudlin or suicidal, just facing facts.

Like many women of my age, nothing I do makes a real difference to anyone any more. Most of my friends are over seventy now, some in their eighties. We all had a purpose, whether it was being a hairdresser like Trudy or being Prime Minister like Teresa May. Well, I'm not sure how much difference she made actually but that's another story. The point is, we had people depending on us. Things had to be done by a certain time. People listened to our opinions.

Most of us have had families too. You need fantastic organisational skills to run a household and bring up a family. It can be like herding cats, getting three children and a husband out of the house in the morning, all wearing clean, pressed clothes, homework done and packed lunches in boxes, then tackling the next batch of washing, ironing, shopping and cooking before they are back again, needing more attention. All that on top of a full time job usually these days.

Some of us have grandchildren living nearby who need help. Some even have children living at home with them again from time to time. The boomerang generation they call them because they keep coming back. But they only want to stay a while until their relationship mends or they get a new one. They cry on your shoulder and spend some of your savings and then leave again.

My eldest has ended up in France and the middle one in Australia. I actually see more of them than the youngest, who lives in London and only comes home when he wants me to bail out his latest business venture. I did think that at least that meant he needed me but on reflection I think I am more used than needed.

A few of us still have husbands of course, requiring more or less care depending on health and disposition. Sandra found having her husband by her side all the time, after their retirement, far too cloying. They had looked forward to taking long holidays together but it turned out she was thinking of walking the Inca Trail and he had lazy days on the beach at Malaga in mind. In the end he had a stroke before they could make a decision. When he died she thought she would travel alone and see all the places on her bucket list but she found she had lost her confidence and fitness and it was too late.

So now we all fill our time with hobbies and try to keep busy. Pat helps out at a charity shop in town and Sandra does a couple of sessions at the local food bank.

Trudy still works a bit, though it's not official. She is a hairdresser, just for a few family and friends these days. I never thought about it before but perhaps that's why she seems so much younger than the rest of us. Or maybe it's because she spends what she earns on beauty treatments. She's never told us explicitly but we all assume she has had the odd nip and tuck.

We all bake and raise money for good causes, or sew or crochet, to try to be useful. I knit a bit but my skills are limited to bobble hats and scarves. You would have to be very cold or desperate to wear anything I've made. Mostly, I meet friends for coffee and lunch or read and watch a lot of TV, when I can work the remote control. That's always a man's job isn't it? It certainly was in my house. John always had the subtitles on TV. Not that he was a fan of foreign films. It was so he could take his hearing aid out and still follow the plot without deafening the whole street. It was months after he died before I found out how to take the subtitles off and then I found I missed them. I had got into the habit of reading the words at the bottom of the screen rather than watching the action.

I do a fair bit of walking and try to keep active generally, hence the class on Friday with the girls. We are trying to live as long as we can, but sometimes, I do wonder what for? Who would miss us really, after a few tears and the funeral tea?

So that comment of Sandra's about being invisible suddenly seemed really pertinent. Once I realised I was pointless and invisible I couldn't stop thinking about it.

What happened next was Richard Osman's fault. We had all enjoyed reading his books about the Thursday Murder Club. The pensioners in those stories are massively underrated by the authorities, because they are old people, too insignificant to notice. I was passing the latest book on to Sandra at our monthly W.I. meeting when I began to wonder what advantages there could be to being invisible.

The speaker that month was droning on about how to make stuffed toys out of old socks and stuffing from duvets. Even her examples looked like aliens from the planet Zog and I knew I would never attempt them. So my thoughts wandered as I looked around at all the women in the room. At least three quarters of them could be described like me. Silver-grey, shortish hair, plump to overweight, depending on how honest I'm being, most wearing glasses, certainly over seventy. If one of us committed a crime, could a witness describe us any more clearly than that? Could anyone pick us out from a line of six similar women? Not that I actually intended to commit a crime.

But I had made a decision. I would look for a bit of adventure in my life. No more sitting and holding the coats for me. Whatever was left of my life, I should live it to the full.

It wasn't long before I had a chance to try out my resolution. On Monday I popped into town. I like to keep a bit of cash on me even though we can flash the plastic at most places these days. I'd been to the bank and was browsing in the market when I saw the man.

He was quite small and skinny with a thin face and pinched features and wearing scruffy jeans and a denim jacket that looked too big for him. He was standing at a stall where they sold mobile phones and accessories. The stallholder was showing a variety of phones to another customer and, as I walked towards him I saw the skinny man pick up something and slip it into his jacket pocket. Then he turned and walked away, heading towards another stall.

I couldn't think what to do for a moment. I hadn't seen him pay for anything, but I suppose he could have, just before I arrived. I looked around but no one else seemed to have seen it. If I challenged him, there would be a big scene, and I would feel so foolish and ashamed if he had paid. But he shouldn't get away with it if he hadn't. He was walking away through the market and I followed along, a few yards behind him.

I've always wondered how easy it would be to follow someone without them noticing. It happens so often in books and in films.   This was my chance to try it for myself.   I followed along as he sauntered through the stalls.   It was easy to keep him in sight.   He didn't act in a furtive or guilty way, even stopping and browsing occasionally.   I did the same, keeping a close eye on him whilst pretending to look at items myself.   As far as I could see he didn't put anything else in his pocket.

After a few minutes he left the market stalls and began to walk more quickly down the main street.   Now I had to hurry along to keep up with him, but he didn't turn round or notice me.   He strode along with purpose, taking a left turn, then a little further on a right, until he came to the door to a pub and disappeared inside.

Now, I am ok with going into the pub in our village on my own when I meet with friends for lunch, or the one we go to in town on Fridays, or one or two other places.   I'm from the generation that broke barriers by going into pubs without our menfolk, shock horror.   I remember my mother being appalled when I told her, as a student in the late 1960s, that we girls met in a pub for a drink quite regularly. We thought we were very daring, and Mum thought we were in danger of being considered 'fast'.   But this pub was the Black Swan.   I had passed it before but never been inside.   It was what my husband would have called 'a drinker's pub.'   There were always a few men, and some women, sitting smoking at tables outside, all of them a bit intimidating, the women with more tattoos than the men, with loud laughter and some pretty ripe language flowing between them.   It was often mentioned in the local paper too because of fights, inside or out.

My first instinct was to walk past, but if I didn't go in I was falling at the first hurdle of what seemed to be turning into my first adventure. I hesitated just a moment, then walked through the doorway.

It took a few seconds for my eyes to adjust to the dim lighting. I looked around at the sticky carpet and battered tables and chairs and saw my man standing at one end of the bar. He was talking to another much larger man with black hair, wearing heavy gold chains and a black sleeveless tee shirt which showed off his bulging muscles and tattoos. There were a few people sitting around the large room but I spotted an empty table in a dark corner, where I could sit with my back to the wall, get my breath back and keep watch on my quarry.

As I watched, Skinny Man took some items out of his pockets. I assumed they were mobile phones but it was hard to see from this distance and in the poor lighting. The big man picked up all the items and moved slightly so I could not see what was happening, but he appeared to be taking money from his pocket and offering it to my man.

"Are you alright, love?" The voice next to me made me jump. It was the barmaid, clearing glasses and wiping the table.

"Oh yes, thank you," I said. "I'm just a bit breathless. I need a drink and a few minutes sitting down." It was easy to play the part of the dizzy pensioner. That's exactly what I was.

"I've not been here before," I said. "Do I go up to the bar to order?"

"You sit there love and I'll bring your drink over," she said. "What can I get you?"

What I really fancied was a strong cup of Yorkshire tea but I wasn't sure they would serve that here.

"Can I have a diet tonic, please?" I said, and she hurried off to get it.

I took out a tissue and wiped my sweaty face, then took the chance to take out my purse and check I had enough coins to pay for my drink. I didn't want to get out the envelope of notes I had just picked up from the bank. All the time I kept an eye on the two men, who were still talking at the bar. In fact, notes were definitely being handed over. Skinny Man seemed to be disputing the amount, but eventually swept the money off the counter and, thankfully without a glance in my direction, he left the pub. Black Vest took the items from the bar and went to join a group at the far end of the room, a bit round the corner so I could not see what was happening now.

Well, that looked like the end of my first adventure. I was in no fit state to chase after my man, and could hardly challenge the group in the corner, even if my legs had not turned to jelly. Maybe I should have raised the alert at what I saw at the market stall after all, but how could I when I had not been sure?

"There you are love," said the barmaid, plonking my tonic on the table. "You sit there till you feel ok." I thanked her and paid for my drink, then took a few deep breaths. My first attempt at fighting crime did not seem to have been an unqualified success.

Chapter 2

Sipping my drink I made an assessment. I was pretty sure money and stolen goods had been exchanged in the pub, but I was not able to do anything about it. I hadn't fully identified the crime in time to stop it or catch a thief. Even if I had called the police, I was too scared of repercussions from the rough and ready group with Black Vest Man. My eyesight being a bit suspect, and my age were against me being seen as a reliable witness. I could imagine getting a metaphorical pat on the head from the police and the case dismissed.

On the plus side, I had learned that I was able to follow someone without being seen. My superpower was invisibility, or perhaps more honestly, insignificance. I could get away with certain actions without being spotted. I just needed to fine-tune how to use that power.

I put my shoulder bag back across my body and walked out of the building, waving a thank you to the barmaid. I had come into town on the bus, as I usually did on market days. It was always difficult to find a parking space, and the bus passed my door anyway. The Black Swan was on the opposite side of town to the bus station and I now had a walk to get back there, picking up a couple of items of shopping on the way. I did not hurry but by the time I got near to the bus station I was ready to sit down again and still fancied that cup of tea. I had never been into the Bus Station cafe before, but I decided this was the time, so I walked in.

As I turned to close the door I realised that a young woman pushing a buggy was coming in behind me. I held the door open for her and she wheeled in the pushchair.

"Thank you," she smiled, manoeuvring the buggy through the doorway and leading a little boy of about three years of age over to a table as the noise of her very young baby's crying filled the cafe. She parked the buggy and removed her coat, telling the little boy to get his colouring book and crayons out of her bag.

As she settled down at the table she lifted the baby out of his buggy and held him in her arms. He immediately started searching with his mouth, obviously smelling the milk that he was so clearly ready for. The young woman took out her purse and opened it, scattering the contents on the table. Only a few coins spilled out, mostly brown ones, and she quickly gathered them again. She draped a light blanket over her shoulder and reached under her tee shirt to discreetly unhook her bra.

The cafe's two assistants had both been busy serving at the far end of the counter as we came in. There was a small bakery section there and they had a little queue of customers. I stood at the counter and looked at the cakes in the display, deciding whether to treat myself. One of the assistants walked across and stopped at the cafe end of the counter.

"It's not table service here you know," she called loudly, glaring across at the young woman, who looked up guiltily.

"Could I just have a glass of water please?" she said. "I get so thirsty when I'm feeding."

"The cafe is for paying customers only!" said the grumpy assistant. "You have to buy something or leave!"

I quickly moved down the counter so I was in front of the assistant. "Tea for me please," I said. "Just a glass of water for the moment for my friend, but she'll be ready for something hot afterwards," and I smiled sweetly, then turned my back to the counter and winked at the young woman who looked down at the baby to hide her embarrassment.

When the drinks were ready I took them to her table.

"Do you mind if I join you?" I asked, sitting next to the little boy. "Hello young man," I said. "My name is Lizzie. You can call me Aunt Lizzie if you like." I held out my hand and he shook it solemnly. He was dark eyed and had a mop of dark brown hair.

"Hi," he said. "My name's Jacob and this is my mummy and my little brother Samuel. He gets noisy when he is hungry."

The baby was now suckling and murmuring contentedly. His mother, blond and blue eyed, was very pretty even with no makeup on. What my son James would have called a 'yummy mummy'. She was plainly dressed and wearing no jewellery except her wedding ring. She held out her hand and I shook it.

"I'm Sarah," she said. "Thank you so much. I just had to feed this one," she lowered her voice to a whisper and leaned forward slightly. "But I don't think I've got enough for a latte afterwards. I seem to be a bit short at the moment."

"Well," I nodded towards the buggy where carrier bags of shopping were stashed underneath in a basket. "It's easy to lose track of what you're spending at the supermarket."

"Oh we didn't go to the supermarket today," said Jacob, with the openness of a three year old. "We went to the food bank."

"Jacob!" Sarah was embarrassed again. "It was my first time," she confided. "We're going through a bad patch."

"Well, we all have those," I told her. "My husband lost his job in the recession during the 1980's. Things were pretty tough for us for a while. I had a baby then too, about 6 months old." Sarah's eyes had filled up. Time to change the subject.

"How old is this little one?" I asked.

"Samuel is eight weeks today and Jacob is nearly three."

"Well they're both little smashers," I said. "You must be very proud of them."

"Oh I am," she said, and her eyes shone as she smiled at Jacob, busy colouring.

I chatted to Jacob about his picture and gave Sarah time to recover.

Soon she lifted her baby onto her shoulder to burp him and drank a little more of the water, then pushed the rest of the glass across to Jacob as she settled to feed the baby on her other side.

"Do you know what?" I said. "I think I need another cuppa. That one didn't touch the sides, I'm so thirsty."

I pushed back my chair and went to the cafe counter. When I came back to the table I was carrying a tray bearing tea for me, a latte for Sarah and a glass of milk for Jacob.

"Oh, thank you!" Sarah whispered urgently, "but I can't take those. I told you I don't have enough money."

I sat down. "Just as well I've paid for them then," I said.

"But..."

"No buts," I said. "There's another glass of water to have first if you need it. It's a long time ago but I can remember how parched that makes you feel," and I nodded towards Samuel, feeding contentedly.

"There you are folks." It was not the grumpy assistant this time, but her more smiley faced colleague. She put down two plates of toasted teacake with jam.

Sarah was open mouthed. Before she could speak I pushed one of the plates towards Jacob.

"Now young man," I smiled at him. "If you can't eat all of that, you can share it with your Mummy. I don't think it's fair that Samuel gets to eat if we don't, do you? We both started to tuck in. After a moment's hesitation, Sarah reached across for one of the pieces of teacake and took a bite. I wondered when she last ate.

Over the next few minutes I found out much more about Sarah's situation. Her husband of five years was a painter and decorator. Covid had robbed him of his job with a small firm and she had been busy having a baby so could not go back to work yet. She was an admin assistant at a medical practice. They had recently fallen behind with the rent but the landlord had been fair and had given Tony, her husband, work decorating another rental property he owned, in lieu of rent. They had a reprieve from being evicted but no income to buy food and no savings left. I remembered being in such a similar situation in the 1980's. And there were no food banks then.

As we talked, and she was distracted adjusting Samuel to a more comfortable position, I pushed my plate across to Jacob's and transferred most of my teacake onto his plate.

"Tony is a hard worker," Sarah said. "He wants to work and has been getting odd days with other firms, but until he finds something permanent, we've applied for benefits. They will take a while to come through though. It's awful. I hate it. But there's nothing else for it."

"Tony would really like to work for himself if he could get established. He's experienced and his work is good. People are always pleased with it. I could do the books. We just need time to build up a reputation."

Samuel was now over his mother's shoulder being burped again, but a sudden rumbling noise told us that something else was happening. Jacob giggled and held his nose.

"Oh no," said Sarah, holding Samuel up at head height and smelling his rear. "I'm down to the last two nappies. I had hoped the food bank would have some but they didn't have his size. I don't know what we'll do after these are gone." She reached into the bag on the handle of the buggy and took out one nappy, a pack of wipes and a nappy sack, then headed towards the toilets at the back of the cafe.

Suddenly she turned. "Jacob, come with me, pet. You must need the toilet too." She looked across at me. "Would you mind keeping an eye on my things till I get back please?" she said.

I nodded. "Of course," I said.

It wasn't until she was disappearing into the toilets that I realised she had left her purse on the table. I picked it up and held it out, about to call her back, but then realised that the door had closed. There wasn't any money in the purse anyway, so I supposed I didn't need to worry.

I sat there for a few moments, sipping the last of my tea. Thoughts buzzed around my brain but soon an idea started to take shape. I looked around the cafe, but it was very quiet and both assistants were busy in the shop. Nobody was interested in me. I was still invisible.

I quickly took two of the twenty pound notes out of the envelope the bank had given me, and folded and creased them into a shape that would fit into the purse. I pushed them right down into the bottom of the wallet side of the purse, as if they had been pushed down there by accident.

As I put the purse down, a card dropped out of one of the other wallet sections. It was Sarah's driving licence. I glanced at it and noted the photo. She was so young and pretty. Then I saw the address. Suddenly another idea popped into my brain.

Another quick check to make sure no one was looking then I took out my mobile phone and quickly snapped a photo of the driving licence. I needed to remember that address and my memory is not all it should be these days. I put the driving licence on the floor and the purse on the table near where Sarah had been sitting, just before Jacob appeared from the toilets, followed by Sarah with a contented Samuel, obviously much more comfortable now.

I started to gather my bags and Sarah put Samuel in his buggy, then helped Jacob to put his colouring things away. As I picked up my shopping I 'spotted' the driving licence on the floor.

"Oh, what's that?" I asked. "Is that yours?

Sarah bent to pick it up. "Goodness," she said. "I am glad you noticed that!" She opened her purse to put the card in, but it snagged on something in the wallet. Sarah looked in and fished out the two twenty pound notes. She looked across at me.

"I could have sworn there was nothing left in here," she said, a puzzled expression on her face.

"Oh, I've had that happen to me," I said, smiling innocently. "They get stuck down in the bottom sometimes." She looked across at me again.

"Well, I must get off," I said. "I've really enjoyed chatting to you. Hi five Jacob." I put my hand in the air and Jacob clapped his against it. "Before I go though, I nearly forgot, let me give you my friend's phone number.   She lives in an apartment block and needs her flat redecorated. She told me there are a few of them looking for a decorator but they can't find anyone reliable. If Tony can do a good job for her, maybe he'll get more business from other people there."

I scrabbled in my bag for a pen and pulled a page from my diary, scribbling down a name and number which she put in her purse with the money. The idea of Tony getting work had successfully distracted her thoughts from how the money came to be there and I beat a hasty retreat, wishing her all the best and dismissing her thanks and attempts to pay me for the drinks and teacake.

"I'll ring my friend and tell her to expect a call from Tony," I said. "You get off home now, but call in somewhere and buy that little one some nappies now that you've found your cash. I know how many they can go through at that age!" I headed off before she could think about it any more.

Chapter 3

Sarah arrived home later that day and placed her carrier bags on the table in the kitchen. Samuel was napping again and Joshua headed straight for his toy corner, happy to play by himself for a while at least. She could hear the shower running upstairs so that meant Tony was back home and getting cleaned up. She started to empty the carrier bags and put tins and packets away in the cupboards, planning meals with some of the unfamiliar brands. Food would be on the table, but maybe the recipes would be slightly different to what they ate normally. No matter. They must look at it as a period of improvisation, making new meals and dishes as well as some that they usually ate.

She had almost finished when Tony came downstairs, looking fresh and clean, but tired.

"How did it go today?" he asked.

"Ok," she said, not wanting to tell him how embarrassed she had felt. This was not his fault, any more than it was hers. The world had changed over a couple of years and lots of people were struggling. They would be alright, so long as they pulled together.

"They were really kind and tried to make it as easy for me as they could. They gave me a good selection of tins and packets but no fresh food of course."

"Well, this might help with that," said Tony, dropping some twenty pound notes onto the kitchen table. "Luan gave me a hundred pounds for two days' work, which is not brilliant but I can't really argue considering he's let us off the rent again this month. The new fence looks good if I do say so myself. We managed to put the garden back into a fairly tidy state afterwards and got rid of the old fence posts and panels. His new tenants will get a blank canvas to work with, though my experience of renters is that they are not gardeners. We are the exception, wanting a proper garden for the children to play in, and space to grow a few flowers and veg."

"That's brilliant!" Sarah was excited. "I found some money pushed to the bottom of my purse earlier today. I don't know how I missed it. Actually, I'm not convinced I did." She told him the story of meeting Lizzie in the cafe and the money being in her purse when she came back from the toilet. "I can't swear she put it there, but I'm sure I looked there really thoroughly before."

"I used some of it for nappies, which we were desperate for, and bought some minced meat and fruit and veg too, so we might be able to save the food from the food bank for a few days. I'll save the money you earned today to go towards gas and electricity bills."

Tony was nodding in agreement.

"Yes, that's going to be the next big hurdle. Let's hope the benefits kick in before then, or I get some more work, cash in hand."

"Ooh, I might have something to help towards that," Sarah was looking in her bag. She pulled out the diary page that Lizzie had given her. "The woman in the cafe, Lizzie, said her friend needs someone to decorate for her . She's struggled to get someone for a while."

She gave Tony the piece of paper with the details of Pat's name and phone number.

"Lizzie said she would phone her and tell her to expect a call from you tonight, after dinner."

"That's hopeful," said Tony. "I'll phone her while you're reading Jacob his bedtime story. It's your turn tonight."

Sarah smiled at him. Jacob was obsessed with Mr Men books these days, not Tony's favourites.

"Luan has some more work for me next weekend. Not decorating or putting up fences this time. He's leased a suite of offices on the third floor of a swanky office building somewhere in Leeds. He wants all his stuff from the office in town moving over there. He says he'll put some fuel in the van and I can move it for him with one of his other lads."

"Not Sami?" Sarah found Sami intimidating.

"No, one of his young lads, just a teenager. Reminds me of myself when I was that age." They both listened as Samuel began to cry. He settled off quickly, but was obviously getting to the end of his nap time and would cry for attention again soon.

Tony turned away from Sarah and smiled to himself as he stood up and walked to the sink, holding a mug under the running tap to get himself a drink.

"Luan was asking after you again." He was deliberately teasing her. "He said there's some famous musical coming to Leeds soon. If you want to go he'll get tickets." He pretended to be asking seriously and waited for her reaction.

"Huh! He didn't mean for you and me I suppose."

"Now you know I'm not a fan of musicals. All that prancing about and singing at the top of your voice, it's not natural!" He couldn't help grinning now. "He says he'll take you for a meal before the show too, give you a good night out."

Sarah grabbed one of Samuel's teddies from his pushchair and threw it across the room at Tony, who caught it before it landed in the sink.

"Don't encourage him," she said. "He's such a sleazeball. Don't lead him on."

Tony knew he hadn't, of course. No way would he want Sarah in Luan's company, but it was fun teasing Sarah.

"Oh, I thought you might like a special night out."

Sarah came round to the other side of the table and put her arms round Tony's neck. "You don't fool me with your teasing," she said. "I'll enjoy a quiet night in with you instead."

They kissed as Jacob came into the kitchen. "Me too! Me too!" he said, grabbing Tony's legs and jumping up and down.

"Ok, ok," he said, bending down to pick up the little boy and holding him so that he could put an arm round each of them. "We'll all have a quiet night in," and they hugged each other.

****

When I got home from the cafe, I phoned Pat and told her I had passed her number to someone who might possibly do her decorating. I asked her to let me know if he phoned and, if he ended up doing the job, how well he did it.

As I sat that evening, half-watching something on TV and sipping a Baileys, I thought about the money from the bank still in an envelope in my bag. I thought about the money that went into the bank each month, from my state pension, my pension from many years as a teacher, and my widow's pension, from my husband's company. I had savings in the bank, money I hardly ever touched, except for times when my son needed 'a bit of a hand please Mum.' He was the only one who ever asked for financial help. My daughter and my other son were both constantly telling me to spend my cash on myself.

"Treat yourself Mum," they always said. "We don't need it and you've earned it. Take no notice of James and his sob stories. It's his own fault when things go wrong for him. It's time he stood on his own two feet."

They were right, of course, about James. I am far too soft with him, though I know I could never see him struggle. But he should be a bit more self-sufficient really and not come running to me as the easy option all the time. That, I decided, was my first resolution for the future.

But what to spend my money on was the question.

I used to tease my husband, John, that I was a cheap date. A cuppa and a cake in a nice cafe was my idea of a treat. I didn't need jewellery or expensive clothes, or luxury cruises. I could afford them now if I wanted them but they still held no interest for me. Going on a cruise as a singleton at my age was particularly daunting. Imagine getting stuck with a 'helpful' couple who insisted on taking you under their wing, sitting at the same dining table each evening being bored by their jokes and persistently escorted on trips ashore. No thank you. Equally, experiencing those fantastic new sights and views without a special someone to share them with would seem pointless anyway.

But not everyone is as lucky with their finances. Meeting Sarah had made me remember that not all people on benefits are skivers and the strivers, those trying their hardest despite life's setbacks, deserve some support. Maybe that was something I could help with, and give myself some pleasure, and even a bit of excitement, at the same time.

The easy way, of course, is to make a donation to charity and I am sure they do lots of good work. But where is the fun in that? And I now knew that I wanted a bit of excitement in my life again, a challenge.

Putting a relatively small amount of money into Sarah's purse had made a real difference to her I hoped, albeit temporarily, and doing it in a sneaky way was quite exciting. Trying to stuff the notes into her hand would have just made us both feel embarrassed. She might even have been offended and would probably have refused. No, doing it anonymously was much better. It had given me a lot of pleasure too. This idea needed working on.

When Pat phoned me later that night, things fell into place.

"Sorry to call so late," she said. It was only nine o'clock but Pat doesn't get out much.

"I thought you would like to know that Tony phoned this evening. He's coming round tomorrow morning at around ten-thirty. He sounded very eager and seems able to get started pretty much straight away." She promised again to let me know how things went. I decided that Tony had passed the first test by making the appointment quickly. Either he really wanted the work or Sarah had pushed him into it.

Now that I had evidence of the couple's willingness to help themselves, I was ready to follow up on the plan I had made when I learned Sarah's address. I took out some writing paper and envelopes and set to work.

The following morning I climbed into my little car and drove to the street where they lived, parking a little way down the road from their house at ten o'clock. Sarah had mentioned an appointment with the baby at the clinic when we had talked yesterday so I was hoping she would be going out of the house this morning too. I pretended to fiddle with my satnav while keeping an eye on the front door. As I sat waiting I thought that even my little car was invisible. No-one noticed me sitting there as they walked by. After a few minutes Sarah came out. She was pushing the buggy and a man, Tony I assumed, followed her out holding Jacob by one hand and carrying a bag in his other.

When you get to our age it can be a bit daunting inviting a strange man into your home and Pat is a bit nervous anyway. I was relieved to see that Tony was dressed fairly conservatively in jeans and a sweatshirt with a short haircut. He was something under six feet tall, slim but not skinny and his sweatshirt bore the words "Only the best husbands get promoted to Daddy." I thought Pat would find that reassuring.

The family walked away, never noticing me or the car. When they got to the end of the street, Tony and Sarah kissed each other briefly, he tousled Jacob's hair, said a few words to him, then crossed the street and turned left while Sarah went to the right with the children in the direction of the local GP's surgery. They looked such a loving family and my heart went out to them because of the trouble I knew they were having.

It was quiet on the street now. This was my chance. Quickly, well as quickly as you can at my age, I got out of the car, locked up and walked to their house. In just a couple of minutes I had pushed an envelope through the door, walked back to the car and was driving away. The envelope had Sarah and Tony's names on the front and the message,

> I hope this helps to tide you over.
> Best Wishes,
> The Invisible Woman.

Inside the envelope was £250.

It was only just after ten in the morning and my first task was completed. A few minutes later I parked outside a supermarket and went in to pick up a few bits and pieces. But I had another purpose in mind as well as my shopping. As I pushed my trolley round I had my shopping list in hand as usual. However, I also had an envelope secreted behind it.

Walking up and down the aisles I took note of the security cameras above me. Usually I didn't think about them at all, but I was acutely aware of them that day. I also noticed other shoppers. It was a quiet time, few people around, mostly older people or mothers with babies, but no children as it was a school day. Everyone was busy and it was easy to avoid prying eyes. After all, I was just another shopper and no one was really noticing me, as usual.

I picked up the items on my list but also a few things that I would not normally buy. Each of these I put back on the shelves after looking at them carefully, as if I had read the ingredients label and decided not to buy. I tried to concentrate on the supermarket's own label foods and cheaper brands, those that I thought people on a lower income would be most likely to buy.

Carefully, I kept my back to any obvious cameras some of the time, practising my moves, but equally making sure that my face could be seen some of the time, so that I didn't look as if I was being furtive. I only had my small handbag with me so I could not be accused of stealing goods. Though it did occur to me that if I were accused of stealing I could play the silly old woman card and would be unlikely to get in any trouble.

After browsing and shopping for a while I found what I hoped would be the ideal spot. Bending to the lower shelves I picked up some own brand pasta. Examining the pack as before I allowed my shopping list to rest behind the packet as I read the ingredients list. When I turned to replace it, I let the envelope slide from my hand so that it was hidden at the back of the pack as I replaced it on the shelf, whilst my shopping list remained in my hand.

The envelope contained twenty pounds and written on the outside of it were the following words.

This envelope contains a gift. I hope you will use it to buy something that you cannot normally afford. If you feel you have enough money to meet your needs, please leave it for someone else less fortunate.
Signed, The Invisible Woman

My heart was beating fast as I walked on, deliberately continuing to browse and shop for a little while before moving to the checkout, paying for my shopping and heading for the car.

As I pulled the car out of the car park I allowed myself a relieved smile. In my handbag I had four more envelopes, two containing ten pounds, one five pounds and one twenty pounds. That meant I needed to make four more visits to shops before I went home for lunch. This was turning out to be as much fun as I had hoped.

Later that afternoon, after putting my shopping away and eating a late lunch, I needed an afternoon nap. As I nodded off I reflected that the day had gone as well as I could have hoped. Of course, the drawback to my supermarket scheme was that I would probably never know who found my envelopes, whether they were strivers or skivers, or even affluent people greedy enough to keep the money anyway. As I had placed the later envelopes I had been confident enough to loiter for a while to see if I could spot anyone finding them but, as far as I saw, no-one had picked up one of my gifts before I left. It was satisfying though, that I might be bringing joy to someone's day, whether needy or not.

Chapter 4

When Sarah arrived home from the clinic later in the morning she noticed the envelope on the doormat. Looking at it, reading the message on the envelope, then finding the money inside, she was astonished. She put the cash back into the envelope, placing it carefully on the kitchen unit at the side of the tea bags. For the next hour, as she played with Jacob and went about her daily routine, she kept glancing across at it.

Eventually, Tony arrived home. He was buzzing after his visit to Pat.

"Hi Sarah!" he called as he came through the door. "I've got a job! Well, only for a few days, but it might lead to more." He was kicking his shoes off in the hall and talking to her as she came through from the kitchen. "The only thing is, I'll need to put fuel in the van tomorrow so I'll need to use some of that hundred pounds."

He looked at her now and saw the serious expression on her face.

"Hey, it's only temporary, love. When this job is done and I get paid, I'll put it straight back, and more I hope."

"It's not that," said Sarah. "Come into the kitchen and look at this." She showed him the envelope and they sat at the kitchen table looking at it and the money inside it.

"Where is it from?" asked Tony.

"WHO is it from, you mean," said Sarah. "I have no idea. Do you? I've been wondering about that since I found it on the doormat. Someone pushed it through the letterbox while we were out."

Tony picked up the notes and counted them. Definitely £250.

"I've counted it ten times already," said Sarah, "and I've racked my brains all the time too but I still can't come up with a name. Who do we know who could afford to give us that amount of cash?"

They were both silent for a while, staring first at the money on the table, then at each other, then back to the money. Tony picked up the envelope, but that gave them no clues either.

"The only person I can think of with that amount of cash to spare is Luan, and this is not his style. He would have made a big thing of it. Anyway, he always wants something for his money. He pays me for work done, it's never a gift. Whoever left this doesn't want anything in return it seems."

"I thought of him too, but I agree, it's not something he would do. Anyway, it's signed the 'Invisible Woman'. Luan would want to take credit for it personally, brag about it to everyone, make us feel beholden to him. But I can't think of any women we know who have that amount of money to spare."

"Mummy, I'm hungry." It was Jacob. The children's television programme he had been watching had just finished.

"Go to the toilet first, then wash your hands," said Sarah. "I've made some soup for lunch." She gathered the money again and slid it into the envelope then placed it back near the teabags. "Let's eat while we think it over," she said. "Nothing's going to change for the next hour."

Tony went to the bathroom to help Jacob and wash his own hands, deep in thought.

After lunch, they took Jacob and Samuel to the park for a couple of hours, but when they came home they were no nearer solving the riddle.

Tony made them both tea and they sat at the kitchen table drinking it, still not able to guess who the envelope had come from.

"I think we just have to accept it for now. Someone's given it to us to help us out, they're not intending to cause us problems, and they want to do it anonymously for some reason. We can't give it back anyway, we don't know who to give it to!" Tony looked at Sarah to see her reaction to his statement.

"I think you're right," she said, cupping her hands round her mug. "I did think we should just keep it, so we can give it back eventually, but there doesn't seem to be any point in that. Whoever it is has given it to us because they know we need help, and we do!"

"The van is due for taxing in two weeks," said Tony. "We had the reminder, remember? I can put six months tax on it and keep it on the road with this money. It might mean the difference between working and not working. Pat, the woman I went to see today, seems to believe there is more work likely in her block. I'll need the van for transport. This is the only way I can see to carry on using it."

They both thought about this for a while then Sarah nodded.

"I think you're right. I think it's a present from our guardian angel, whoever he or she is and we have to accept it as well intentioned and use it wisely. Keeping the van on the road makes good sense."

She reached for Tony's hand and gave it a squeeze, then stood up, picked up the envelope and gave it to Tony.

"Right," he said. "I've told Pat I can pick up the paint she wants on Monday morning. I have that gardening job for Mrs. Cook at number 46 in the afternoon but if I start Pat's decorating on Tuesday it should be finished by the weekend when I'm working for Luan, moving stuff to his new Leeds office." They were both smiling. "Let's hope there is some spin-off work from the job for Pat too." Maybe things were going to get better after all.

****

I was woken from my nap by a call from Pat, who was thrilled that Tony had popped round to look at the job as promised, bearing colour charts and samples. She had found him polite and comfortable to be with. In fact, she seemed quite smitten by him.

"He has the most beautiful eyes," she said, "and he's such a proud dad. He saw photos of my godsons on the windowsill and he brought out ones of his two boys from his wallet to show me. They look like lovely little fellows."

He had quoted a fair price and arranged to start on Monday, assuring her that he could move any furniture that needed shifting out of the way. He promised he would make sure her carpets etc were well protected and he could get the materials she wanted on his trade account. He would provide bills, he said, to show what he had spent so that she could see what his labour costs were. All those things are important when you are an older woman, on your own. It's always a bit worrying getting tradespeople in, especially if they are unknown and not recommended by someone who has already used them.

That evening I had a celebratory glass of Baileys and tried to think of ways to improve on my schemes.

Finding other cases to help like Sarah and Tony would be my ideal but coming across people by chance was a random exercise. Also, it was not sensible to give away hundreds of pounds at a time, to all and sundry. Until I had cases that seemed in specific need, and I could be pretty sure their need was genuine, I would not be making that size of gift again. But, in the meantime, I would continue to make a couple of envelope drops each week as I picked up bits of shopping. Placing five in one day had been a one-off experience. Too risky, and too expensive to continue at that rate, on a daily basis, thrilling though it was. Doing it in different places, like pound shops, and even charity shops, and on different days of the week, would spread the net and help to protect my anonymity.

****

The following week I was very tempted to say something, or at least hint what I was doing, to the rest of the Friday gang at our lunch, but each time I almost blurted something out I thought better of it. Pat would think it was far too dangerous and worry I might be arrested. Sandra would blab when she had one gin and tonic too many with the locals at the pub on quiz nights and Trudy might think I was boasting.

I was acutely aware that not everyone has the same amount of disposable income as me. Trudy could be pretty scathing about people with workplace pensions, having been self-employed all her life. We'd had one or two difficult conversations about it in the past. She had a dig at me and I had bitten-back comments I could have made about her tax free income as a mobile hairdresser. She made no secret of the fact, especially after a couple of drinks, that she declared only a limited amount of her cash income. It had been her choice, I felt, to spend it as she got it, and not invest in a pension for her twilight years.

In the end, we hedged around the subject if it came up. I didn't want it to look now as if I was showing off about the amount of cash I could afford to give away. So, I carried on without telling anyone and accepted the fact that I would not get any feedback about my mystery gifts.

After a couple of weeks had gone by, I was pleased to learn that Tony had been as good as Sarah had promised. I made a point of asking to visit Pat after he had finished. Pat's lovely, in fact, maybe too lovely. She probably would not criticise even if the job was a bit of a mess. I wanted to see for myself if it was as good a job as she said. Pat was delighted to show me.

"Come round tomorrow," she said, as we enjoyed our Friday lunch. "I made a banana cake yesterday and it will be at its best then."

I was pleased to see the flat did look as beautiful as she had claimed. Chatting over coffee and cake (which was at its delicious best) I also gleaned a bit more information.

"Tony was really good at keeping the mess down and clearing up after himself," Pat said. "I've had some work done in the past and they've left it all for me to clean and tidy, and one man covered my sofa with paint splashes too."

I was cheeky enough to ask about the price.

"I've had three quotes for the same job and they were all more expensive than him, and they couldn't promise how long it would be before they would come. To be honest, I gave him a bit of a bonus and he was so grateful. He told me they'd had a difficult patch financially, but somebody had helped them out the day he came round to give me the quote. He has been able to put diesel in his little van and tax it so he could pick up the paint and stuff and get it here."

"Oh lovely," I said. So that's how they used my money. An investment to make a living. Excellent.

By the time I visited Pat several neighbours in the complex had booked him, after seeing the job he had done for her. He was already working on a neighbour's flat that day. One of the care workers who regularly visited the place had asked him for a quote for her house too. It seemed that his dream of being self-employed was coming true. Pat's flat did look good and I was so pleased, well, relieved really. It's always a risk when you recommend somebody, but Tony had not let me down.

As I was leaving I decided I ought to get him to take a look at my lounge and the hall and stairs. Seeing Pat's newly decorated walls had made me realise how shabby and old fashioned my place was looking. If I wanted Tony to do it, I should get in quick if he was getting so busy.

As luck would have it I saw him as I crossed the car park to my car. He was putting his things in the back of a little van. It seemed silly not to say hello and ask him to pop round. I was just about to walk over and introduce myself when someone else approached him and I stopped in my tracks. It was the man from the pub, Black Vest Man.

I stopped walking and took my phone out of my bag as if I had just had a message. Tony did not know me and Black Vest Man had probably not seen me that day in the pub, he had been too busy negotiating with Skinny Man. It was easy to keep an eye on them as I wandered slowly over to my car, pretending to look at my mobile phone. I climbed into the driver's seat and continued to watch.

Tony did not seem pleased to see this man any more than I was. He stood behind his van, head down, not making eye contact while the other man loomed over him. I am not an expert on body language but it was easy to tell that the man's whole attitude was threatening and when he grabbed Tony's arm I held my breath.

Tony looked up then, looking him straight in the eye and shaking his arm free. Whatever was being said, he was not in agreement and was not afraid to stand up to the bigger man. I sat in the car watching until Black Vest Man finally stalked back to his car and drove away with a squeal of tyres. Tony watched him go, then turned to his van and continued loading his gear away.

Now was my chance to speak to him. I walked across the car park and said his name as I approached.

"Tony?" I said, "are you Tony, Sarah's husband?"

Tony looked up, his face clouded, obviously still thinking about the confrontation he had just had. When he saw me his face changed. "Hello," he said, and he smiled questioningly. "Are you a friend of Sarah's?"

"Well, we met a while ago in the bus station cafe," I said. "I am Lizzie. I'm a friend of Pat's at number twelve."

"Oh, you are the woman who helped her that day when the assistant was so snotty about her breastfeeding and not buying a drink. And you gave her Pat's number for me to call about doing her decorating." He held out his hand. "I need to say a big thank you, you have been a life-saver, in more ways than one." Maybe more than you know, I thought. "She was so low, that day, having to go to the Food Bank. There just didn't seem to be any light at the end of the tunnel." He squeezed my hand.

"Well," I smiled at him. "Things seem to have picked up now, at least work wise?"

"It's been brilliant," he said. "Pat's job has led to so many others here and spin off work. I can't thank you enough for suggesting it."

"Pat's so pleased with what you have done," I said. "In fact, that's where I have just been. She's been showing me how beautiful it looks. That's why I've come over actually. I was wondering if you could give my lounge and hall, stairs and landing a bit of a facelift."

"Of course," said Tony. "Shall I come and have a look at it and then I can give you a quote and see when we can book it in?"

"That's great," I said. An idea occurred to me then. "In fact, why don't you bring Sarah and the children? I would love to see her and the boys again."

"She'd like that," he said. "She keeps saying that she wished she could thank you for your help that day, but she had no way to contact you." He put his hand in his pocket and pulled out some small business cards. "This is my number, and I can write Sarah's mobile on the back of the card. He took a pen from his pocket too and scribbled a number on the back. "Phone us tonight and I'll tell her to expect a call. I'm out pricing another job after the children's teatime, but she knows my diary better than I do so she can arrange something with you. We'll look forward to it." He beamed and shook my hand again.

"I'll do that," I said, "and I'll look forward to it too."

I hesitated then said, "I couldn't help seeing you seemed to be having a bit of trouble with the man who was talking to you just now. Is everything alright?"

"Oh him," he said, "he is a nasty piece of work. He works for our landlord."

He paused, as if thinking what to say next.

"He wants me to do something for them but it's not a job I want. Don't worry. I can handle him." He smiled and closed the van doors. "I'll tell Sarah to arrange something and look forward to seeing you soon." We shook hands again, got into our vehicles and drove off.

I obviously was not going to find out anymore just then, but maybe when they came round to my house I could glean more information. My feeling was that Tony was being put under pressure to do something illegal, or at the very least, unsavoury. If I could help him avoid that, I would.

It was lovely to talk to Sarah when I rang her that night. She was thrilled at how much work Tony was getting, though she did say that meant he was not available for a few weeks to work on my house. We arranged for them all to come around at the weekend, when Tony officially had the day off, but could combine giving me a quote with a social visit.

Chapter 5

The next Tuesday I did another envelope drop while shopping at the supermarket. I had still not had any feedback from previous drops, although I had done it for almost a month now. When I got home I put the kettle on and sat down to enjoy a cup of tea while listening to the local radio. What I heard made me stop with the cup half way to my lips.

The presenter was explaining how the woman he was about to interview had been having a difficult time but things changed when she was shopping in her local supermarket.

"Hello there, Julie," he said cheerily. "I think you've been having a bit of bad luck recently. Can you tell us about it?"

"Well Jonathan, it's all a bit of a mystery, but wonderful in the end. My washing machine broke down about two weeks ago and I just didn't know where to turn. I couldn't afford to get it mended or replaced but there's four of us to wash for, me and three kids. I needed to get it done but I couldn't do it all by hand."

"Oh that sounds like a nightmare, Julie. What did you do?"

"Well for the first week I had to take everything to my mum's. Bless her, she let me do my washing there, but I had to carry it back to my house on the bus to get it dried at home. Believe me Jonathan, a load of wet washing is heavy to get home on the bus!"

"Sounds like a difficult time for you. So how did you solve it?"

" I didn't really solve it myself. I was shopping in Lidl for a few essentials and I found an envelope in between the cereal packets. I thought it was just a bit of scrap paper at first, but it had some writing on it."

"Can you remember what it said?"

"Better than that, I can read it out to you. I still have it. It says 'This envelope contains a gift. Please use it to buy something you need. If you do not need it, please leave it for someone else to use.'"

"Well that's intriguing! What was in the envelope?"

"That was the amazing thing. When I opened the envelope, there was £150 inside! I couldn't believe it!"

"Wow! That's fantastic. What did you do next?"

"Well, Jonathan, when I picked myself up off the floor, I went home and rang the repair man. He came round the next day and repaired the washing machine. It only needed a small part and he had it in his van so he could get it sorted there and then. It's as good as new."

"That's fantastic news. But do you know who put the money there? Was there a name on the envelope?"

"That's the reason I phoned in. I've no idea who it was from. It was just signed 'A Well Wisher.' I wondered if I could ask your listeners if they know who it could be and get a message to whoever it is to say how grateful I am."

"Well there you are folks. There's a kind person out there. If you can help us solve the mystery of who it is, please phone in." He gave the radio station's contact details and moved on to play more music.

I was intrigued. I had never put that amount of money in any of my envelopes. I listened carefully as the presenter read out the wording on the envelope again, a little later in the programme. It was almost the same as I put on my envelopes, but this envelope came from 'a Well Wisher'.

As the programme went on the presenter asked several times if any listeners knew anything about who it could be, or if anyone else had found similar envelopes. I was as curious as him. Someone else was leaving random gifts. I waited impatiently, not daring to walk away from the radio to do anything else. Eventually he had news.

Two other people called in. One didn't want to be interviewed live on air but had given the information that she had found an envelope containing twenty pounds in a local pound shop. She had been thrilled as it had meant she could get much needed new shoes for her little girl. The second caller was happy to be interviewed.

"My little boy and I found an envelope with ten pounds in it when we were shopping in the supermarket two days ago. Thomas wanted to buy sweets of course, but I pointed out that that would be quite a lot of sweets which would be bad for his teeth! In the end, we compromised by getting sweets, but taking most of them to the Food Bank here in town."

Both these envelopes were mine, and the radio presenter pointed out that they were signed differently to the first one, by 'The Invisible Woman.'

What a wonderful result. Even if these were the only two people who had used their gifts as productively as this, I felt the scheme had been successful. But who was the mystery Well Wisher who was copying my idea? No one rang in with further information, though the presenter and his callers made the point that there did appear to be two different people leaving the envelopes in various stores around the town. He asked for anyone else to contact him if they had any other information but by the end of the programme no one had.

A couple of days later I bought the local paper and the main article on the front page was all about the mystery givers. There was a picture of the first woman I had heard interviewed on the radio and a third person, a man, told his story of finding an envelope containing five pounds. There was great speculation about whether there were two givers, working together or independently, or just one, writing different messages on the envelopes. No one was able to offer any solution to the question of who the donor was.

I chuckled to myself and thoroughly enjoyed the speculation I and the mystery donor were causing. Of course, I was as intrigued to know the identity of the second person donating gifts as anyone else. Speculation was high, but no actual identification seemed likely as yet.

I decided that I needed to lie low for a while and not make any more 'drops' till the excitement died. The possibility of being discovered was much too likely at the moment. Shoppers and assistants were all on high alert, watching everyone. I was due to visit my daughter in France for two weeks anyway, leaving at the end of the following week. I decided I would have a break until I got back and hope that by then people would have forgotten about it.

When we had lunch on Friday, I knew I had made the right decision. All the other Friday girls were full of the news and trying to guess who it could be. I joined in with a degree of deception I did not know I could master. The Scarlet Pimpernel would have been impressed.

"I wonder if it's anyone we know," said Sandra, pouring over the paper before passing it on to Pat.

"Someone with more money than sense, I'd say," said Trudy. "Why else would they give it away like that?"

"I think it's a lovely idea," said Pat. "I think it's giving lots of pleasure to people, and a helping hand. It's a bit like being a secret Santa."

I grabbed the opportunity to support the idea.

"Yes, wasn't the original story of St. Nicholas about a man who went round his town dropping off presents for children at the doors of houses? Didn't he work anonymously too? A much better idea than what happens these days, when children expect rather than hope for their Christmas presents. People feel pressured into buying more and more expensive gifts nowadays, often ones that are not appreciated or even wanted."

The conversation turned to the subject of unwanted Christmas presents.

"OOh yes," said Trudy. "I can't believe the number of people who think that I might still use real hankies with my initials, or a bit of lace in the corner. That idea went out with our mother's generation. Even my old Ma used tissues in her later years."

"And why do people buy me chocolates, when they know I am trying to cut down on the calories? I put them in the drawer and try to resist them, but they shout at me till I take them out and open the box, then end up scoffing the lot in a big binge," said Pat.

"My pet hate is tea towels," said Sandra. "I'm not a domestic goddess and anything for the kitchen is wasted on me, but tea towels! Really! I must have one from virtually every seaside resort or stately home my family has ever visited."

They looked at me expectantly, waiting to see what my least favourite present was.

"For me, the worst thing is those gift sets of smellies. You know what I mean, soap and matching hand cream in a box, or bath bombs! I don't even have a bath these days, I always shower. They're always in some cheap perfume that you don't like too, and they've probably been given before to at least one person who then tries to pass them on again. If they don't give them to me as a present they will end up donating them as a raffle prize at the W.I."

There were general nods of agreement and some slightly guilty looks. None of us could meet each other's eyes as we had all been guilty of that one.

The food came and the subject changed to something else. I breathed a sigh of relief that I had avoided any difficult questions.

****

Sunday was the day that Sarah and the family were coming. I took out a few toys from the cupboard, things I always kept handy for visitors with children. I have a theory that there are no naughty children, just bored ones. Sarah had sensibly provided something to keep Jacob happy in the cafe when we met. I hoped he would enjoy some of the old fashioned toys that I still had from my children's childhood. I put out a boxed set of matching cards, two jigsaws and some toy cars. They usually go down well, so I hoped he would like them too.

When the family arrived there were hugs and smiles all around. Sarah tried to thank me again for my help in the cafe and starting Tony off on the route to self employment. We had coffee and cakes with juice for Jacob then I cuddled

Samuel and he gazed at me with that puzzled look that young babies give you.

We chatted companionably for a while and then I handed Samuel back to his mother and Tony and I started discussing what I wanted him to do to the lounge to make it feel modern without losing the traditional look I still loved.

My house is an old 'gentleman's residence', built in 1905 with big rooms, lovely high ceilings and bay windows. Tony said it was a job he would need help with, but he had an ex work colleague, semi-retired, who would work with him. We measured up and discussed colour schemes, then moved on into the hall. The more we talked the more I could detect a very slight accent. Or was it a dialect, I could never remember the difference. My daughter was the one with the ear for language. I wondered where he was originally from but we were too busy talking about how to decorate the hall for me to concentrate on his accent now.

"It's a beautiful house," he said, admiringly. "Don't you find it a bit big though, for just you? Have you never thought about downsizing?"

"Thought about it but never decided to do it," I said. "It's the house my children grew up in and when they visit, which is not as often as I would like, it's the house that they bring my grandchildren to. I suppose what I'm saying is that it's my home, not just a house."

"I know what you mean," said Tony, as we walked up the stairs. "I still miss my home, where I lived as a child. I've lived in several houses since but none of them have felt permanent. Sarah and I were saving for a deposit on our own place, but that's all gone, since our financial problems. We are getting back on an even keel now." He paused. "At least we don't owe any rent and we can pay our way in future."

He had reached the landing and stopped in front of the framed photographs displayed on the wall. I came up the last stair and stood beside him.

"This is my family." I pointed to a photo of an older man. "My husband John died two years ago now." I went along the row. "This is my eldest, Emma, at her graduation. Then there's Dan at his. There isn't one of James graduating of course, he's the black sheep of the family and dropped out in his second year. This picture of him was taken one Christmas as I wanted him on the wall even if he wasn't wearing a cap and gown. The row underneath is the grandchildren." I stopped. I was getting carried away, doing the proud granny bit. Tony had stopped in front of the picture of Emma.

"This is your daughter, Emma?" he repeated. I came back to stand beside him.

"Yes, she's older now, of course. Married and living in France."

Tony was staring at the photograph. He suddenly turned to me, his face serious. He put his hand on my arm. "Did your daughter work with Kosovan refugees in the summer of 1999?"

"Why yes! How did you know that?" He was silent. "She had a summer job with people that were flown into Britain from refugee and prison camps in Macedonia. The Local Authority did a sort of summer activity scheme for the children and she was employed on that."

"I remember," he said. "We went skating and swimming, to museums sometimes, and played rounders and football on the grass." He looked back at Emma's picture. "I have a photograph of the workers with us children, all of us happy and smiling. Emma is standing next to me with her hand on my shoulder." His eyes were brimming with tears. "I was eight years old. I am Arton, Tony in English."

"Oh my word!" My hand shot up to cover my mouth. "Are you the boy. . . ? She told me about a boy. . . whose brother . . ." I stumbled over my words and stopped, suddenly realising that this was a question I could not ask.

Tony nodded. "My brother was killed in our apartment in Pristina," he said. "We were all there when the men came. My mother, my sister, and us two boys. He was thirteen, my brother, my hero. They said they were police, but they were not like the police you know. They were looking for my father but he wasn't there. They kept asking us where he was but we didn't know. We couldn't tell them even if we had wanted to."

Tony stopped talking to look down over the bannister. We could just hear Jacob and Sarah talking as they did a jigsaw in the kitchen. Tony continued very quietly now.

"My brother tried to protect us, tried to be the man of the house. He told them they should get out of our home. They pulled him away from us and made him sit in the corner, tied his hands behind his back." He stopped to take a deep breath. "Then they put a plastic bag over his head and said they would take it off when my mother told them where our father was. But she didn't know."

I could not move my hands from my mouth. I didn't know what sound might come out. Tony had tears streaming down his cheeks.

"Emma was the first person I talked to about it." He touched Emma's picture then wiped tears from his face with his hand. He took another deep breath. "The interpreter had to translate, of course. I only had a few words of English then. We were at the skating rink and I was having such a great time and I suddenly realised I wished that Hasan was there having a great time too. I ran across to Emma and the interpreter and kept thanking her for bringing us here, telling her how much fun it was and how I wished that my brother could be here to enjoy it. So she asked me where he was. She thought he must be at one of the other camps. Lots of families had been split up like that. But I told her what had happened to him"

"She told me," I said, "that evening when she got home. She told me. He was the same age as Dan and you are the same age as James. She could imagine Dan trying to protect our family if it had happened here."

By the time Tony and I went downstairs we had blown our noses on lots of loo roll and given each other several hugs. I was going over to France the next week so promised I would tell Emma all about him and his family too. I knew how pleased she would be to hear that he was making a success of his business and his personal life. Somehow we managed to get back to thinking about decorating. We finished measuring and deciding on colour schemes then went back to join Sarah and the boys.

Sarah looked up questioningly as we entered and I could see that she had been wondering why we were taking so long. Although we had tidied ourselves up she could see that we were both a bit red rimmed around our eyes and I saw a look exchanged between husband and wife that showed they would talk about this later, without the boys present.

We all had another drink while Sarah fed Samuel, then, with a date arranged for a month hence to start work, we said goodbye with more hugs all round.

That evening, sipping my usual Bailey's, I talked to Emma and told her the news. She was delighted to hear about Tony - she still called him Arton - and glad he was still in the UK.

"Things are rumbling even now in Kosovo you know, Mum," she said. "We don't hear much about it, because there are so many other more volatile situations that dominate the news. Did he say what the rest of the family were doing? I know most of the refugees were only over here for a short while. They wanted to go back as soon as things were safe, a bit like the Ukranians do now. But some applied for asylum, if it wasn't safe for them to go back. Arton's family must have been allowed to stay here. I wonder if they found his father." I was cross with myself that I had not thought to ask that.

"Do you remember the three older boys I worked with, Mum? Even after the summer scheme had finished I kept in touch with them for a while. They were all a couple of years older than me, and going through the application process for asylum. I helped them with forms and stuff. Two of them had family connections in Italy and wanted to be relocated there. They were ordinary boys from well-off families, who had been picked up when they were out shopping for trainers. They seemed so much like my friends at university. But there was another boy who started to get sucked into the black economy. He found himself work in town but was not specific about exactly what he was doing or who he was working for. It was all a bit iffy. I wonder what happened to him."

I was sure I would be able to find answers to some of these questions when Tony started working in my house, and Emma promised to look through photographs she had taken of the summer scheme, while I was over with her, so that I could take copies for Tony. Our conversation turned to plans for my travel and holiday with her. I tried to focus on looking forward to my family visit and push the horrors of war and ethnic cleansing out of my mind for the time being.

Chapter 6

A month later I was home again after a lovely holiday and was getting back into routine. I met the girls for our keep fit class and realised how much I had over indulged and under exercised on holiday. I was back on the diet coke and had a healthyish soup lunch.

I was surprised to find people were still buzzing with curiosity about the envelopes. The local paper had reported that a woman finding one more of my gifts had come forward, saying she had put the twenty pounds she found towards getting a senior rail card. This would enable her to make more visits to her family who lived a distance away. That struck a chord with me and I was pleased to have been party to aiding that. Another gift from the 'Well Wisher' had also been found, this time of £100. The finder just said it was going to be used for something near to his heart, but didn't specify exactly what and wished to remain anonymous. Sandra's guess was that he meant cigarettes and he could keep a packet in his top pocket.

"Wish I could find one of the envelopes," said Trudy. "I'd get a dose of botox." She fingered the almost non-existent vertical groove between her eyebrows and the rest of us all automatically felt the same spot on our own faces.

"I don't think that's what it's supposed to be for," said Sandra.

"Why not?" Trudy was defensive. "If it's a gift you can spend it on whatever you want."

Pat hesitated. "But it's not essential is it? I know we would all like to look younger but this money is supposed to be for things we need, not just what we want."

"You know you look younger than the rest of us anyway, you glamour-puss," said Sandra. "The least you could do if you find one is share it with us so we can all treat ourselves to a facial and manicure each." There was general laughter and nods of agreement.

I did not tell them that I had an envelope containing £10 in my bag at that moment. I was heading to browse the local charity shops for bargains after lunch. I know I can afford to buy new things, and I do, but we all love a bargain don't we? Anyway, recycling is good for the planet. So I was hoping to hide the envelope at the same time, perhaps among the books. But in the end that didn't happen. Something else demanded my attention.

After leaving the Friday group, I cut through one of those bargain shops to get to the main street. As I was passing the section selling tea and coffee a man was putting a box of tea bags back on the shelf. I suddenly remembered I needed tea myself, so as he moved off I picked up the box. Behind it was an envelope bearing the usual message and signed 'A Well Wisher'.

The man was heading away down the aisle. Quickly, I grabbed the envelope and pushed the tea bags back on the shelf, then hurried after him. He was just outside the door as I caught up with him.

"Excuse me." I had tapped him on the shoulder and spoken before I really knew what to say. "Er, I think you left something." He turned to look at me and I held out the envelope. For a moment he did not speak.

"I saw you actually, so it's no good denying it." As I said this I realised I could be wrong. Perhaps he had found the envelope, decided he wanted to leave it for someone else and was just putting it back. I tried to do a quick assessment of him without making it too obvious. He was about my age, with a pleasant face and grey hair and beard. Not skinny but not fat, and probably about five foot eight or nine. He looked 'outdoorsy', with a healthy tan and wearing a wax cotton jacket and light brown cord trousers.

I suddenly realised that he seemed to be assessing me too, before he spoke. For some reason I blushed. I thought for a moment I was having a hot flush but that phase of my life was over quite a while ago. This pink colour creeping up my neck was definitely caused by a slight feeling of self-consciousness. I reached in my bag for my envelope, placing it on top of his. His eyes moved to look at it then back to my face. Slowly, he smiled, his eyes sparkling and one eyebrow raised slightly then he put his hand into his coat pocket and pulled out another of his envelopes.

"Snap," he said. We were both too surprised to speak for a few seconds then he said, "I think we need a drink. Do you want a coffee or something stronger?"

I would have loved something stronger, a brandy would not have gone amiss. But, as my cheeks were already feeling flushed and I was driving anyway, I suggested the little coffee shop just down the road and we made our way there. We introduced ourselves as we waited for the waitress to bring our drinks.

"I'm Lizzie," I said.

"I'm Titus," he said, shaking my hand. "Named after Titus Salt, not Titus Andronicus, before you ask. My mother was born in Saltaire."

"I've heard about him," I said. "He was quite a character. Is that where you got the idea of philanthropy?"

He smiled. "Maybe. But I know someone who found one of your envelopes and I liked the idea. Not long after that I had a bit of a win on my premium bonds and I decided I would like to share my good luck. But it was you who gave me the idea of how to do it." We paused as the waitress put our coffees on the table. He took a sip then spoke again. "So, what's your motive?"

"Similar to you I suppose," I said. "I'm not exactly rich but I have enough and there's so much hardship around I felt I could share what I have. But I'm a bit more cynical than you. I felt that not everyone who found my gifts would necessarily be in need of help, so I keep mine to smaller amounts. Then even if they are greedy types they only benefit a bit, and anyone really in need will be glad of a bit anyway."

"Good philosophy," he said. "I think I got rather carried away with the idea at first and maybe didn't think it through as well as you."

"I also have a selfish motive though," I admitted. "I wanted some excitement in my life and hiding the envelopes is such fun. It's been lovely getting the feedback recently, on local radio and in the newspaper. I never expected that I would know what had happened to the money, but even little amounts have been well used or given someone something positive to enjoy in pretty depressing economic times. Of course," I paused for another sip of coffee, "the people who don't come forward might be spending it on drugs or something I suppose, but they wouldn't get far with small amounts."

"You're right, of course. I was quite impulsive with the first couple, but I've cut the amounts down myself recently. That envelope you have has fifty pounds in it which is the most I do now, and not that often either."

"Oh!" I said. I had forgotten that I still had the envelope and quickly fiddled in my bag, bringing it out to slide it, face down, across the table. I felt very furtive, like a spy passing on information. "You'd better have this back so you can put it somewhere else."

"Thanks," he said, leaning back to put it in his coat pocket, then giving me an appraising look. "I must say though, I would never have described you as an invisible woman." He smiled. "I would notice you anywhere."

I felt myself blush again, for the second time in many years and was suddenly glad I had put my make up on this morning. I often don't bother these days but if I know I'm meeting Trudy I feel I have to make an effort or I feel a bit of a frump.

We chatted over a second cup of coffee and got to know a bit about each other. Titus had been married, but had no children. "My fault." he said, "I worked for a news agency based in London. We lived down there but I was away a lot and it just never seemed the right time." In more recent years, when his wife became ill, they had moved back up north where he was originally from and he had worked as a sports reporter on a regional newspaper. That way he did not have to travel so far or be away for so long.

"Claudia died four years ago," he said, nodding as he looked down at his coffee cup. "So now I'm on my own. I still do a bit of work here and there to keep busy. Reporters are a bit like policemen. They are always on the job and never really retire," he said.

By the time he had walked me back to my car in the car park we had arranged to meet for a pub lunch two days later. I couldn't believe I had said yes when he suggested it. I had never been interested in anyone else since John had died. Well actually, since I had met John as a young woman. Why I suddenly felt comfortable with this man was a surprise, but I did, there was no denying it. In fact, more than comfortable, there was a frisson between us that I had never thought to feel again. I hoped I was not being a silly old woman.

As we shook hands beside my car I noticed two men talking in the doorway of a shop at the other side of the car park. Before I thought about it I said out loud "Oh it's that man again."

Titus turned round to look. Black Vest man was still in his sleeveless tee shirt despite being outside in this cold spell. It must be a macho thing. He was talking to another man, slighter and more smartly dressed, in his mid forties at a guess and smoking.

Titus turned back to me and shot me an acute look. "Do you know those men?" he said.

I was surprised at his sharpness. "Not really. Not the man in the suit at all in fact. A friend of mine, Tony, knows the other man and I saw them together once. I don't think Tony likes him, in fact I think he's being put under a bit of pressure to do something for him and my friend is saying no." I stopped, not wanting to say too much about Tony.

"Hmm. Tell him to stay away from them. They're both bad news," said Titus, keeping his back to them.

"Who are they?" I couldn't help asking.

"The man in the tee shirt is Sami. He's lower down the chain than the man in the suit. His name is Luan. He has a property empire mostly in the seedier parts of town but he's buying houses in more salubrious areas too recently. He has a finger in a lot of pies with very unsavoury fillings, but he fronts it all with legitimate properties and businesses." I remembered John saying once that people who are self-made millionaires have often started by stealing their first thousand pounds, then moving into acceptable investments as they become wealthy. Titus took a glance over his shoulder. He was still holding my hand after our handshake and as he turned back to me he squeezed it and looked at me with a serious expression. "I mean it Lizzie. Tell your friend to steer clear."

We parted then so I didn't ask him how he knew all this information and we didn't discuss the men again when I met Titus for our pub lunch. We enjoyed each other's company and were both relaxed and content just to get to know each other a bit better. He seemed to have lived quite an exotic existence compared to mine, based around sporting events. I admitted to being jealous when he told me that he went to so many of the important matches and competitions that I had only watched on television.

"You lucky thing," I said. "I keep promising myself that I will visit Wimbledon. It's definitely on my bucket list, but I'm running out of time and have not managed it yet."

"So what else is on your bucket list?"

"Oh, lots of different sporting events. I love to watch show jumping, and did go once to the Horse of the Year Show with my daughter when she was about sixteen. But that was years ago, so I would like to go there again."

"I like cricket too. I got into it when my sons played for the village team. They were always short of someone to score, so I ended up being press ganged into doing it one week. That helped me understand the game more and I really got into it and did it regularly after that. John and I used to go to watch Yorkshire play at Headingley sometimes, but more often he went with a group of pals. A bit of a boys outing, so I couldn't go along."

"What football team do you support?"

"Ah, there you have me. Football is not my game I'm afraid. I've watched the odd England match when it's on television but I'm not an enthusiast. I would rather watch Rugby Union any day. What's that old saying? Football is a game for gentlemen played by hooligans and rugby is a game for hooligans played by gentlemen."

Titus grinned. "Oh well, and you were so nearly perfect. I'm a Man City fan myself, though I don't get to the games much these days. But I admit I like to watch Rugby Union myself too." He continued to eat for a minute then said, "I'm actually at the England match at Twickenham in a couple of weeks." He looked up at me, watching my reaction.

"You lucky man!" My eyes were wide with surprise and envy. "That's definitely on my bucket list. I've been a fan since the World Cup match in 2003, when Jonny Wilkinson scored the winning points with his drop kick."

"I only watch these sports on television of course. And you can't always do that these days unless you subscribe to about five different things like Netflix and Sky Sports. If you're a girl on a budget, like me, you have to choose which you can or can't subscribe to. It was a sad day for me when they stopped showing cricket live on Channel Four." I sighed and ate another mouthful of my lasagne. "It must be wonderful to see games live."

"One of the perks of the job," he said. "I'm not actually covering the match at Twickenham this time but I have been invited as a member of the press." He paused in thought for a few moments as I ate and he sipped a glass of red wine, then said, "Would you like to come with me? I can get you in as a guest."

I stopped eating and looked up at him again.

"We could get there and back in the day, on the train. Might be a bit of a long one, getting back a bit late, but it is do-able." I was glad that he had not suggested an overnight stay. I didn't know how I would have handled that.

"Are you sure?" I was very excited at the thought but didn't want to cause him any problems.

"Well, you might have to pose as my camera crew I suppose," he said thoughtfully. "Are you good with a camera?" and he grinned.

Chapter 7

The next meeting with the Friday girls was a bit awkward. I was still buzzing with excitement and knew I couldn't keep my forthcoming outing secret forever. I wanted to tell them about my new friendship anyway, but couldn't explain how we had met. In a way, I wanted them to meet Titus and approve of him, but I worried that they would think I was foolish, having what Pat would call 'a gentleman friend' at my age. Sandra would caution me about scam relationships, being asked for my money or bank details. Trudy was the real worry though. She has had a series of boyfriends over the years and we joke that she is a bit of a man eater. We once asked her how she found so many eligible men.

"Well, some are more eligible than others," she admitted. "But they are out there if you know where to look."

We waited expectantly. "You meet surprisingly helpful men in B & Q if you hang about looking lost," she said. "They're queuing up to show their macho skills with a power tool."

"How on earth did you think of that?" Pat said.

"I went in to get a new toilet roll holder, because mine had come off the wall. It's too small a job to get anyone in to do it but I had no idea what to do. I was walking around looking lost when one of their 'helpers' asked if I needed anything. Before I knew it there were three hunky men with tool belts arguing about the best way to fix it on the wall. All three of them offered to come and do it for me."

You can see why I didn't want to introduce her to Titus. I thought he might be smitten. I decided to wait a bit longer before I said anything.

Meanwhile, Tony had turned up on Monday with his mate David, as planned, and started work decorating my house. It was a messy process and I stayed out of the way, just being on hand to provide cups of tea as needed. They had their radio just slightly off station, which seems to be compulsory for all tradesmen, and at a volume that made talk redundant. Tony was never still and never without David, so, apart from a quick chat when he arrived the first day, to confirm that Emma had been delighted to hear about him and his family, and had sent photographs and news, we had not had time to exchange any real information.

By Thursday great progress had been made, but David could not work after lunchtime that day, so Tony was working alone. We took the chance to have a private chat. I spread some photographs on the kitchen table, the ones Emma had printed out for me to give to Tony.

"Emma wondered if this was the one you mentioned to me. There's a crowd of you and here's Emma." I pointed at my daughter in the photograph. "Is that you standing next to her?"

Tony was looking at the photos one by one, but put the others down to concentrate on the group shot. "Yes, that's me and my sister is at the side of me. These older two boys I don't know so well. They were single young men, grown ups as far as I was concerned. I think one of them had family in another country and they were trying to get to them. Maybe they were relocated, but I can't say for sure. I was only young and a lot of the important stuff went over my head really, or they kept it from me if it was bad news."

I had to ask the question that Emma and I had wondered about. "Tony, Emma wanted to know if you ever found out where your father was. She's really hoping so."

Tony smiled and took a photo from his wallet. "This is all my family together, after we were reunited. This was taken the day we moved into a house, here in England. My sister is living in Sheffield now. She trained as a teacher and married another teacher she met in the first school where she worked. She has two children like me."

"My mother looks so happy here," Tony's smile faded. "But about two years later she was diagnosed with cancer. She fought it, she fought hard, because she wanted to look after us, but she died when I was sixteen."

"My father had already died by then, when I was fourteen. He never recovered his health when he came out of the prison camp."

His father looked gaunt and hollow eyed in the family photograph. I couldn't imagine what horrors he might have experienced. Emma had told me that many of the refugees had TB. She had seen some of them, those who were flown to Britain later than others. Usually this was because they had been arrested and kept for some months in the prison camps.

"They were like walking skeletons," Emma said. "They had been beaten and tortured. They usually came to us after being in the hospital, depending on their needs. Arton's father was not found by the time the summer scheme ended. I suspect that means he was one of the last to be brought out so probably in a bad way when he got to England, if he got here at all." She would be pleased to know he had been rescued and had spent some years with his family, even if his health and that of his wife had not been good.

Tony took a deep breath and looked at the photos again, deep in thought.

Then he shook himself and smiled again. "We've had such opportunities here, and our parents got the best care they could have had." He looked at me. "Tell Emma that Britain welcomed us and helped us better than we could have ever imagined. They gave my father asylum because his life was in danger if he went back, so we were all allowed to make new lives here. We will be grateful forever." He pressed my hands in his. "Forever."

"You must tell her yourself," I said. "She insists that you have her contact details and get in touch. She is planning on coming over in a couple of months and hopes you can meet up."

He smiled. "I'd like that," he said, "I'd like that a lot."

While I made us a sandwich and tea, Tony continued to look at the photos. When I sat down he pointed again to the group shot taken at the camp.

"This boy, this young man, is still here too." He pointed to a tall young man in his early twenties. Emma had pointed him out to me when we looked at the pictures in France. He was the one slipping into the black economy when the scheme finished at the end of the summer. He had seen other opportunities developing in his world and wanted to stay here and take what chance threw at him.

"He stayed?" I questioned, and Tony nodded.

"His name is Luan. He's my landlord."

Luan. The man Titus and I had seen talking to Sami in the car park.

I had suspected as much of course, when Titus had described him as having a property empire with some better properties recently. That was my chance to warn Tony that I had heard Luan and Sami were bad men. I couldn't say who had warned me about them. I had to be careful. I hadn't known Tony all that long and he had a relationship with Luan that went back to a time of shared trauma.

"Look Tony, maybe this is none of my business but I have to tell you something. A friend of mine was talking the other day about a man he knows of called Luan. He said he has lots of property in this area. Could this be the same man?" I was certain it was but it was difficult to explain how I knew.

"It has to be," said Tony. "It's unlikely there are two property magnates in this area called Luan." He was smiling, unaware how concerned I was feeling.

"My friend thinks he's a really bad man, Tony. I don't know you very well but I don't think you are like him. I hope he isn't getting you involved in anything that might get you into trouble."

Tony nodded thoughtfully. "I know he is mixed up in some bad stuff, but he has a good side too. He was always kind to me at the camp. Remember my father was not around for quite a while and my brother was dead. He was very protective of me."

"Since I left school I have occasionally done odd jobs for him and he's never asked me to do anything shady. Well, not until recently," he admitted, "and I've refused that."

"What does he want you to do?" I knew I shouldn't ask, but I had said it now.

Tony sighed and shook his head. "Oh, he doesn't mean it. He knows I won't do it anyway." He paused, then must have decided to get it off his chest. "He thinks I can use my work, being in people's houses, to steal stuff for him, or at least pass on details, alarm codes and when people are out at work and so on. He has people like Sami who would sell stolen goods. They would go in and do a burglary later, after I had gone."

"Tony!" I sat up straighter and looked at him. "You wouldn't!" I was thinking about my jewellery upstairs.

"No way!" he said. "My values are very different to his. Apart from the fact that I would probably be the one getting caught somehow, despite what he says. Actually, it's his disregard for my safety that's made me trust him less these days. I'm beginning to suspect that he's gone further to the dark side than I realised."

He picked up a photo of his wife and children that he had brought for me to pass on to Emma. "I would never do anything to jeopardise my family's security. Or be anything other than the best role model I can for my boys. Like my father was for me."

"Luan was good to us, renting us the house at a fair rate, and letting me work in lieu of rent, when we got behind. Sarah didn't know he is our landlord till we were struggling with rent. He's put a bit of pressure on me recently with this idea, but I think that is more Sami than Luan."

"What does Sarah think about them?" I asked.

"She thinks Sami is a bully and Luan is a creep," he grinned. "He keeps suggesting I let him treat her to a night out at the theatre. He once heard her saying she loved to go when she was younger and he keeps offering to take her. He knows the theatre is not my thing even if we could afford it and there's not much chance of that at the moment."

I was quite shocked. "And what does Sarah think about that?" I asked.

He grinned. "I think you can guess!" he said.

I left it at that and Tony went back to work.

That evening I called Titus and told him everything we had said. "Keep working on him Lizzie. I can't stress enough what bad news both these men are. Tony really needs to keep away from them." I felt quite scared by his urgent tone. He seemed to know more than Tony about Luan's 'dark side'.

"How do you know so much about them?" I had to ask. Had he had trouble with them personally or did he get his information by word of mouth?

"Like I told you, I still have friends in journalism," he said. "They're keeping an eye on what he's up to and most of it is pretty nasty."

I thought for a few moments. "Maybe I can get to him through Sarah," I said. "Sounds like she really doesn't trust Luan. I'll arrange to have coffee or lunch with her soon and see what I can do." We turned the conversation to our forthcoming trip to Twickenham.

Chapter 8

It turned out that I didn't manage to meet Sarah until after I had been to the rugby match.

It was a wonderful day; a fantastic experience altogether. We spent quite a bit of time together over the two weeks leading up to the day and became more and more comfortable in each other's company. I looked forward excitedly to my outing, but made sure to ask about appropriate clothing. There's nothing worse than turning up to a formal dinner in casual clothes and vice versa. Footwear can be a particular problem. I was fortunate enough to go to a Buckingham Palace Garden Party once, with John. He had done a lot of work with the Prince's Trust and lots of people from that organisation were invited to one of these wonderful 'thank you' parties. Luckily it was a hot summer day and I wore a comfortable floaty dress (I still have it in my wardrobe) and a hat of course. Luckily I chose to wear sandals with a wedge heel. It was pure good luck in my case but a lesson well learned. I watched some poor women teetering around in stilettos with their heels sinking into the grass, sometimes getting stuck or in one really unfortunate case, breaking off altogether.

These days I struggle to stand too long in high heels, but hate looking dumpy in flatties, so it's always a bit of a compromise. Anyway, it turned out we would not have far to walk, travelling pretty much door to door by train and taxi, and having seating for the game. Although we did stand when we 'socialised' in the bar with lots of press and famous personalities from the sports world. I felt very special, wearing a lanyard with my security pass on it. I was welcomed by everyone who knew Titus, which was pretty much everyone, and generally felt like royalty for the whole day. Of course, it was made even more special by the fact that it was a really exciting game and England won.

Titus had picked me up in the morning and parked his car near the station so he was able to give me a lift home too at the end of the day. I was almost asleep, but still buzzing with excitement and thanked him profusely. He even walked me to my door and we had a first kiss as we said goodnight. Very chaste of course, but it still felt daring. A bit strange after all this time never having kissed anyone but John, except on New Years Eve perhaps, and a bit tickly, him having a beard, but very nice. Trudy would no doubt have laughed at my innocence, but that's how I am, I can't change that.

Almost a week later I was still buzzing about the fabulous time I'd had and decided I had to tell the Friday gang. I would never manage to keep it a secret while I was having lunch with them. I broke the news about Titus himself first.

"You sly old minx," said Trudy. "How long have you been keeping him hidden?" We were in the pub as usual after our gym session. I was a bit vague about answering that, and about how we met, just saying we had bumped into each other in town.

"Have you got pictures?" asked Pat. "What does he look like?" I started to get my phone out while we talked.

"You need to be careful, Lizzie," said Sandra. "Has he asked you for any money?"

"Far from it," I said, as I passed my phone over to her. "In fact, I struggle to get him to let me pay for anything."

"Wow," said Sandra, squinting and holding my phone at arms length to get the photo into better focus. She had forgotten her glasses again. "He looks a lot like Johnny Wilkinson."

"Oh, sorry, no," I took the phone back. "That is Johnny Wilkinson. Titus took me to a big rugby match last weekend and we met some former England players. There's one here of me with Lawrence Dalaggio too," and I proudly held out the phone to show it round.

Of course, I had to explain that Titus had been a sports reporter and we got into one of the special hospitality venues at Twickenham on his press pass. Everybody there seemed to know him and I had met lots of famous faces. I finally found a picture of him with me, holding a glass of champagne each.

"Actually, Jonny Wilkinson took that one for us," I said proudly, as the phone was passed round. "I kiss the phone every night now and put it under my pillow!" I joked. We had all agreed years ago that Jonny was dishy and any one of us would be happy to have him as our toy boy.

"Titus is not bad himself," said Trudy. "A bit of a Sean Connery type in his more mature phase. I wouldn't kick him out of bed."

I grinned sheepishly. "It's not got that far yet. But I must admit, I really do like him, and it is lovely to be taken out and given treats."

"Good for you, girl," said Trudy, passing my phone back. "So when do we get to meet him?"

I knew that would be asked. "Well, it's early days," I said. "Let's see how it goes for a bit. You can be an intimidating lot, you know, and I don't want to risk frightening him off just yet."

We parted after lunch with predictable farewell comments from each of them.

"You will be careful, love, won't you?" from Pat as she gave me a hug and a worried look.

"Just don't give him any money or access to your bank details," from Sandra and "Get in there kid, don't let the grass grow!" accompanied by a lascivious wink from Trudy.

I decided that it was time now to tell my children. Unlike the Friday girls, they were unlikely to bump into Titus and me together, but I still felt that I was keeping a secret from them. I wasn't sure how any of them would feel about me having a special male friend. They had all been so fond of their dad.

I called Dan first. "Sounds like a nice bloke Mum. If you like him, that's good enough for me. Just keep a sensible head on your shoulders," was his reaction.

James could only hear half of what I said. It sounded as if he was out with mates in a noisy bar. "Go for it Mum," he shouted above the din. "Do whatever makes you happy!"

When I called Emma I got a bit more of a grilling. After asking his full name, Titus Brookes, she wanted to know how we met. I bent the truth slightly. "It was an accident. He dropped something while he was shopping. I picked it up and gave it back to him. We got talking and ended up going for a coffee."

"So what did he do?" she asked. "I'm assuming he is retired now?"

"Semi retired," I said, quoting what Titus had told me. "He was the sports reporter on the Yorkshire Gazette, and before that he did the same job based in London, but covering matches all over the world. He still does bits and pieces of work now but I'm not really sure what." I told her all about the visit to Twickenham and having VIP treatment there.

After a few more questions she gave me her blessing, like the boys, just cautioning me to take care things didn't go too fast. She also said she would like to meet him when she came over in a few months. I breathed a sigh of relief and felt I could enjoy my romance with an easy conscience.

Now I could get on with talking to Sarah and getting her support to keep Tony away from Luan's influence. Tony and David had done a brilliant job of redecorating my house and moved on to other jobs so I invited Sarah over to have lunch with me and see what they had done. Jacob was on a playdate for the afternoon, so she had only Samuel with her. That made it easier to bring up the subject of Luan without little ears flapping.

We started by looking at some of the photos that Emma had sent and talking about the experiences that Emma and Tony had shared, skating, bowling and so on. Sarah knew all about the terrible time Tony's family had experienced before coming to Britain, but she never knew Tony's mum or dad. They had died before she met Tony. Then I passed her the group photo and pointed to the young man that I now knew was Luan. I confessed that I had heard he was still around and that he had a bad reputation.

"Yes," said Sarah, "He's done very well for himself but I suspect it's at the expense of some people less fortunate. I didn't know till recently that we are renting our house from him. He hides behind various business names and we dealt with a reputable letting agent. I think he is trying to become 'legitimate' now but I have heard terrible things about what he is involved in behind the scenes."

"I am a bit worried about Tony being friendly with him," I confessed. "Tony obviously knows Luan from way back and feels that he owes him something for his help when they were both younger. But I have a friend, Titus, who says that Luan is a really bad man and Tony should steer clear of him."

"Oh dear," said Sarah. "Yes I know Luan is into some bad stuff. I used to hear more on the grapevine when I was working. Tony has done odd jobs for Luan but I'm sure he doesn't do anything seedy. Luan has moved into some new premises recently. He's decided he wants some of the offices smartening up, giving a new 'corporate image' and he's got Tony lined up to do some night shifts for him, so the offices can still be used during the day. Tony helped him move his equipment from his old premises into the new office not long ago and they were having a look at it and deciding what to do."

"I understand he has tried to make a bit of a play for you?" I tried to phrase things as tactfully as I could. I didn't want to offend Sarah.

"Oh that!" she said. "Well, yes. He does get a bit of a pest about that. He keeps trying to get me on my own. He does it in a very jokey way, trying to make out he's asking me out for a treat, to the theatre or for a nice meal. But I'm not falling for it and Tony just laughs because he knows I'm not taken in. Don't worry about me," she smiled, "I can handle him."

Samuel woke up at that point so we were distracted and the subject changed. I hoped that I had said enough but not too much.

****

The next few weeks settled into a bit of a routine. Titus and I continued making envelope drops, separately, and at infrequent intervals. News about them had faded. What's the saying about yesterday's news being tomorrow's chip paper? Although I don't think it applies anymore, health and safety rules meaning that newspapers can't be used as food wrapping these days.

We also had regular outings. It sounds silly to call them 'dates' at our age, but we enjoyed going for meals or to the cinema, and to a couple of concerts. I found him easy to be with, good fun. Amazingly he seemed to enjoy my company too. Far from feeling ordinary and dumpy, when I was with him I felt special, interesting even. For the first time in years someone was listening to my opinion, enjoying my sense of humour. It was a heady mix and a feeling I hadn't had for years.

Much as I loved John our relationship had become quite staid over time. I think it happens to many marriages. John died a couple of years before we would have celebrated our golden wedding anniversary. I suppose being with the same person, day in, day out, things are bound to become pretty routine. If I'm honest, I think I gradually adopted a slightly subservient role too. John had quite a high powered job and was a bit of a larger than life character. I preferred being in the background. He definitely dominated in a group, happy to voice his opinion and be the centre of attention, while I became less confident and outgoing.

Titus seemed to be bringing back the old me.

Once we had enjoyed a meal at his house and twice a lunch then an evening meal at mine. It was such a pleasure having someone else to cook for. Meals alone are such solitary things, I don't bother setting the table but usually eat on a tray in front of the television for company. With Titus, I had not made a big thing of setting the dining table, that would have seemed a bit over the top, as if I was wanting candles and a romantic evening. But sitting enjoying a home cooked meal at the kitchen table while we talked felt just right. We even did the crossword puzzle together after our lunch. He was quite good and could answer the questions I got stuck on. We made a good team.

One evening, we were at the kitchen table again enjoying a coffee together after another meal, when we heard the front door open. We both looked towards the hall and listened. The front door slammed, then there was the sound of a bag being dropped on the tiled floor.

"Hi Ma! Anyone at home?" called a man's voice.

Chapter 9

"James!" I stood up and went to meet my youngest child as he came towards the door into the kitchen. I am always pleased to see any of my children but James's visits have sometimes had an ulterior motive, so my stomach does tend to flip a bit when he arrives unannounced. I walked towards him and we hugged.

"This is an unexpected visit," I said, standing back to look at him. "You look well, love." He did. A bit pale, but I think James spends a lot of time indoors, day and night. He's not an outdoorsy type and spends his leisure hours at the pub rather than the gym.

"You too Ma," James said, looking me over. "Really well in fact. Do I detect a bit of a sparkle here?" He came round the kitchen door and spotted Titus. I felt like a teenager caught by her father with her latest boyfriend.

"James, this is the friend I told you about, Titus Brookes." Tutus stood up and held out his hand. James stepped forward and shook it.

"Well, well well, Titus Brookes. I'm so glad you're here sir. I came up specially to meet you when I found out who you are. I would have recognised you anyway from the photos I've seen. It's a privilege to meet you."

"James, be serious," I said. To the best of my knowledge, James had never called anyone 'sir' since he was at school. I turned to Titus. "He's joking. James has a rather individual sense of humour. I phoned him the other day and told him a bit about you and he's making it sound like . . .like. . . I don't know what, really, but don't take any notice. And what do you mean about recognising Titus?" I turned to James again. "I didn't show you any pictures of him."

James looked at me, then at Titus, who was looking a bit uncomfortable. He looked at me again, then back to Titus. "She doesn't know, does she?" he said. "Well, I really hope you have some coffee left in the pot Ma, because we have some talking to do."

A few minutes later we were all sitting at the kitchen table with fresh coffee in front of us. James was smiling at me and Titus in turn. "Shall I start, or do you want to say anything?" James asked him. Titus lifted his hand slightly, meaning James should speak first.

"So . . . I got a call last week from Emma. She told me you had a new friend . . . Titus here." He waved his hand in Titus's direction. "It wasn't a surprise, of course, as you had phoned me before. I couldn't hear what you were saying because I was on a night out and it was pretty rowdy, but I got the gist and it was fine with me. You're a grown up, more sensible than me, so why would I even think of interfering. So long as he treats you right, any man you choose is ok by me." He took a sip of his coffee. "Oh that is good."

"Anyway, Emma has inherited your genes so she hadn't just taken Titus at face value. She checked him out on social media."

"Titus doesn't do Facebook or Twitter," I said. "Like me he thinks the internet can be dangerous."

"Too right Ma," James grinned. "You really don't need to tell me that. I'm the one who cleans up your laptop every time I come home and steers you away from using the internet whenever I can. Remind me to check it over tomorrow, by the way," he added.

"Anyway, as you say, there was nothing on standard social media, but then Emma looked on Linkedin and googled him generally."

Titus did not meet my eye. He was leaning with his elbows on the table and his hands to his forehead looking down at his coffee mug.

"What's Linkedin?" I asked. I had vaguely heard of it but just assumed it was another social media site where people shared pictures of their lunch, or dogs doing silly tricks.

"It's a site where people post their c.v.'s. A sort of employment agency where employers and employees can find out about potential jobs and people to fill them. People can get in touch with each other if they think they have work ideas in common."

"And? I told you that Titus was a reporter for the Gazette." I was really nervous now. Was Titus not what I had been led to believe? Maybe Sandra and Pat had been right. But everyone knew him in the press section at the rugby match. Even famous people were happy to shake his hand and seemed to think well of him.

"Don't look so worried Ma." James reached out and grasped my hand. "It's not bad news. Emma found out that your friend here has indeed been the sports writer on the Gazette. That he was widowed and has no children. All correct, as you had told Emma. It was his earlier life that was a bit of a surprise. When he worked out of London."

Titus looked up now. "In my defence I never lied about that. When I talked about working in London I didn't specify my role and I suppose your mother just assumed I was a sports reporter then too."

I looked from one to the other. "For goodness sake, will one of you tell me what you did do then?"

James looked triumphant. "This man," he waved his hand towards Titus again, "was a reporter for the news agency Reuters. They are a well respected news source world wide. He was one of their roving reporters, working all over the world from time to time, but especially in Eastern Europe."

"James, I know who Reuters are," I said. "I'm not a complete idiot. Why didn't you tell me?" I looked at Titus for an answer.

"This man," James was on a roll. He knew he had something special to tell me. "This man has worked in some of the worst war-torn regions of Europe," said James. "He covered the breakup of Yugoslavia, the Bosnian war, Milosovic and his ethnic cleansing in Kosovo, you name it." I could hear the admiration in James' voice. "He won awards, Ma for reporting from the hot spots. He got shot twice, for goodness sake!"

I was looking at Titus and suddenly realised my mouth was open. I shut it quickly. He was looking at me too, but apologetically. "They were both only slight wounds. I don't talk about that time much. There were some pretty horrendous things going on, not something to chat about over dinner with a friend." He gave James a hard stare, but James was ploughing on. There was more he had to tell me.

"Well, once I read that, I had to delve a little deeper," he said. "We all know that some of these Reuters guys do more than report on stuff. All unofficial of course. They carry information and arrange things, they act as go-betweens and smuggle people from one country to another. I had to find out if this man here did anything like that. So I looked into my special sources." James paused to add to the drama. Titus was sitting up straight now and watching him intently.

"What I found out blew my mind. It's not generally known, these things are hush hush and all that, but he's done some pretty amazing stuff. Among other things he somehow brought fifteen people out of Kosovo, some of whom had been incarcerated for several months. Reporters and broadcasters Ma, news people, who had been prevented from sending reports out to the world; arrested, tortured and goodness knows what. Some of them were in hiding in isolated places, others were in prison camps where they'd been sent to disappear, the ones who survived at least. No-one knows how he did it but it must have been at great personal risk. He's a legend among the few people that know about these things."

We were all silent for a few moments. I needed time to take this all in.

"And now it's my turn to talk." Titus had been staring at James as he spoke. "That information is not generally available. It's not supposed to be available at all. You didn't find that on Wikipedia. I need to know how you got it."

"Me too," I chimed in. My voice was an octave higher than normal and came out as a squeak. I was feeling out of my depth and needed to understand what was happening here. I cleared my throat and started again.

"Me too. There seems to be a lot I need to know."

"Ah, fair comment," said James, nodding at Titus. "I do owe you an explanation. You too Ma, there's a few things you don't know about me."

My mouth was open again, I realised. I shut it quickly.

James sipped some more of his coffee and settled back in his chair. "Well, you know I've always been a bit of a whizz with computers?" I nodded. "Well, after they kicked me out of Uni I . . ."

"Whoa!" I interrupted. "You got kicked out of Uni? I thought you just left because you didn't think it was your thing?"

"Oops! Sorry, perhaps I didn't make that quite clear."

"What did you do? Were you missing lectures or getting bad grades?"

"Well, yes, all of that." There was hesitation and a bit of embarrassment. "It's what I did about it that they really didn't like."

I raised my eyebrows and waited.

"I hacked into the university computer systems and upped my grades and attendance. It was stupid, I know. They were obviously going to notice that this kid who they'd never seen was getting the best grades ever. I've learned a lot since those days."

Somehow I didn't think he meant he wouldn't do it now, just that he would be better at it. He had the decency to look a bit shamefaced.

"Yea, well, anyway, after that I tried a few things, always internet based, trying to set up my own business or sometimes working for other people. You know that Ma because you've bailed me out more than once." I nodded and waited for more.

"A couple of years ago I had a big break. Do you know that there's a section of the police force that deals with cyber crime?" I nodded, yes I was vaguely aware.

"They approached me. They employ people like me to look for the bad guys, block viruses, trojan horses, trace scam artists and ransom attacks, stuff like that. They call them the men in white hats. The bad guys are the men in black hats and the ones that have done bad stuff but are willing to come and work for the good guys now, they're grey hats."

"So are you one of the men in white hats?" I hoped so.

"Let's just say my hat is mostly white but there might be a few spots of grey sprinkled here and there." James grinned and sipped his coffee again.

"Wow," I said. This was a lot to get my head around. About both of them.

"Wait a minute," said Titus. "There's more." He was looking intently at James. "He didn't get the information about me as part of a police investigation."

"Bingo," said James, "You know your stuff. Last year I was headhunted by the big guys. You know who I mean. The ones nobody talks about. The ones who don't officially exist. The ones you have to sign the official secrets act to join." There was silence. "That's all I can say folks. In fact, if I was talking to anyone other than the two of you I wouldn't have said this much. This can't go out of this room."

There was a long pause, then Titus leaned across the table and put his hand out. "It's a pleasure to meet you James," he said. James shook his hand.

"It's an honour to meet you, sir."

I took a deep breath. "I don't know about you two but I need something stronger than coffee. It's not every day you suddenly find out that your son is some kind of internet super sleuth. Or that the man you've been having quiet lunches with is actually an international undercover agent. " I walked through to the sitting room and poured myself a large glass of Baileys. The two men followed me. "Help yourselves to something," I said, waving a hand in the vague direction of the drinks cupboard.   I started to turn towards the sofa, then turned back and grabbed the Baileys bottle, putting it on the side table next to me as I sat down.

"Whisky?" said James as he and Titus followed me.

"Any brandy there?" asked Titus.

"There's a cheeky bottle of Calvados here."

"Sounds good to me."

They sat nursing their drinks, casting concerned glances at each other and at me.

It was a few minutes before anyone spoke. My head was spinning with the information I had just been given. Suddenly something occurred to me and I turned to Titus.

"Titus, have you been grooming me?!"

"What?!" he said.

"Not exactly grooming I suppose, that's not the right word. What I mean is, I can't get my head round this Kosovo connection. Did you know before you met me that I know Tony and he knows Luan? Are you plotting something and using me as a go between? Or did our worlds just happen to collide?"

"I feel pretty much the same about you knowing someone with young James' connections," Titus said. "The chances of anybody being able to find out about my past in that kind of detail are pretty remote. So the answer to your question is no, Lizzie. I was not planning any of this. If you remember, you pointed out Luan to me the first day we met."

"I will confess that I am keeping an eye on him and what he's up to, and I have made some of my contacts aware of some stuff I know about him, but nothing to do with you."

"And as for Tony, all I know about him is what you told me. Mostly that he did your decorating for you."

"I'm sorry, should I know who you are talking about?" asked James.

I explained who Luan was and who Tony was, then had to explain how I came to know Tony and his connection with Emma. Then Titus filled us both in on some of the more unpleasant aspects of Luan's business. I was shocked to find how deeply entrenched and depraved the man was. He had involvement in drugs, which I had expected really, but also trafficking and modern slavery. I couldn't believe that someone walking round the streets of our little town, a businessman gaining a reputable reputation in some areas in fact, was actually a crime lord.

"My colleagues have not picked him up so far because we want to follow the chain higher up as well lower down. We need a way in to get to his contacts, bank accounts, business records and so on. I think that, so far, he is so sure of himself that he has incriminating stuff pretty accessible. He's not as high tech as he should be in this day and age. But if he gets a whiff of anyone investigating he will make everything disappear. He's already hiding behind his new squeaky clean connections."

James waved his glass of whisky in the air. "Excuse me," he said, "have you forgotten that I wear a white hat? What exactly do you need?"

Titus looked at him seriously. "Do you think you could get clearance to look into things if we can find a way in?" he said.

"I can check it out," said James. "I imagine my bosses might be interested to hear what you and the guys you work for know already and see where we go from there."

"Excuse me," I said. "I have just one thing to say about this. Whatever plan you two hatch, I want to be part of it." And I poured myself another Baileys.

Chapter 10

Titus insisted the first thing we needed to do was okay things with their respective 'organisations'. I insisted the first thing I wanted to do was warn Tony to stay away from anything to do with Luan.

"He's doing some decorating next week at Luan's new offices. He has to be there several nights running, working in one office after another. I don't want the place to be suddenly raided by your colleagues and Tony to get arrested for something that has nothing to do with him."

Titus exchanged a look with James. "Tony is going to have access to Luan's offices with no-one else around? Are these the offices in Leeds that he took a lease on recently?"

"I think so," I said. "Sarah mentioned he had to drive to the city but at least he was travelling at night so the traffic would not be bad."

"This is a suite in a big block in the city centre," Titus explained to James. "He had men moving stuff across from his old premises in the town centre here a while ago now. It's all part of his glossy new image. I checked it out. There's a security guard on duty but he's an older man. It's a boring job so he'll probably nod off for an hour or two or be easily distracted by something he's watching on his phone. There's a service entrance at the back of the building."

"If you're thinking what I think you're thinking," I stopped, not sure I was actually making sense. I'd had quite a lot of Baileys. "What I mean is, it sounds like you're wanting Tony to get more involved, not less."

"That might have to be his decision, Ma," said James, "not yours. He's a big boy and he knows that some nasty things happen in this world. He needs to be given all the information and then he can make up his own mind. Can you arrange for us all to meet, preferably tomorrow as it sounds like this is too good an opportunity to miss?"

I agreed to make a phone call and moved through to the kitchen to get my mobile. James followed me and put his whisky glass in the sink. "I'm heading off upstairs to email a few people now, see what I can fix up. Am I ok using my usual room tonight? I assume you two love birds will both be in your room?"

"James!" I was quite shocked. "We're just friends!"

"Come off it Ma. This man is pretty special, you're never going to find anyone better than him, and he's obviously besotted by you. I've seen the way you two look at each other. Get on with it. You're only young once!" and he kissed me on the cheek and started to head upstairs. He turned round in the doorway. "Anyway, he's just poured himself another Calvados so I don't think he's planning on driving anywhere tonight!"

I took my phone back to the sitting room and sat next to Titus while I phoned Sarah. I didn't explain what I wanted to talk to her and Tony about but I did say it was something urgent and that I wanted to talk to both of them and bring a couple of other people with me.

"Are you alright Lizzie?" asked Sarah. "You sound a little strange."

"Yes, fine Sarah, but this is really important and we need you and Tony together after the children are asleep."

"Okay, see you tomorrow night."

I put the phone down and turned to Titus. We were both silent for a minute.

"You should have told me," I said.

"In fairness Lizzie I had no idea of your connection to Luan through Tony. You just told me that you had a friend who knew him. I told you to warn him off as strongly as I could."

"But I told you about him coming from Kosovo and you still never talked about being over there and all that other stuff. I had no idea about any of that."

"But for James you still wouldn't have. It's not something I'm supposed to talk about at all. And it's all in my past anyway.

"Hardly!" I was annoyed. "You're obviously watching Luan and reporting on him - who to I'm still not sure - and it appears that you're looking for an opportunity to do more than watch."

He took my hand. "I did tell you reporters and policemen never retire. If we get a tip off about something, we can't help investigating."

"Lizzie, you want to make the world a better place. I've not known you long but I know that's true. No-one can put all this stuff right. Governments and agencies who specialise in fighting this sort of thing can't put it all right.. If we do find a way to stop Luan and maybe even some of the people further up the chain, someone else will take their place. More people will be trafficked or become addicted to drugs or whatever bad stuff these despicable people decide will make them the most money. But that doesn't mean we should stop trying. If we can see a way to make life just a little bit better for even one person, we have to do it."

I sighed. "I need to sleep. My head's spinning with all this. And I've had too much to drink."

"Of course, I should go." He stood up.

"Don't be silly," I said. "You've had too much to drink too. You can't drive tonight." I stood up as steadily as I could but was feeling a bit wobbly. "I really do need to sleep though. Can we do that?" We were both on our feet now and he looked into my eyes.

" Whatever you say, Lizzie. Whatever you say."

****

The following morning I came downstairs to make tea and take it back to bed, to find James already sitting at the kitchen table working on his laptop.

"Morning love, you're not usually an early bird." I stood behind him and put my arms round his shoulders. "You certainly sprang some surprises last night." I sat down at the table to wait for the kettle to boil.

"Sorry. I haven't been able to say anything before but I'm afraid excitement got the better of me yesterday. I wouldn't have said anything now if you hadn't met Titus."

I moved over to the kettle and reached for two mugs.

"Anyway, I've got full approval to take this as far as I can and work with Titus on it. Let's hope that Tony comes in on the deal too. My techie guys are sending me some things that might be helpful. They're coming by special delivery so they should be here today."

I turned, with the two mugs of tea in my hands, heading for the stairs.

"Don't keep him too long Ma. There's a lot we need to talk about."

I shot him a glance. He was bent over the keyboard, grinning.

Most of the day was spent looking at maps and drawings of the office building. I didn't follow a lot of what was said, but gathered that Titus was able to give James good initial information with which James could then use his expertise to research further details online. A lot depended on Tony's reaction to the situation and we would find that out before the end of the day.

Sarah and Tony's house was small but neat and tidy. They were obviously curious to know what this was all about so we got straight down to business after I had introduced everyone. First Titus explained that what we were discussing had to be secret. He told them how he had information about Luan and the sort of things he dealt with. Initially, Tony was rather dismissive. He knew that Luan had some dodgy dealings but still felt quite protective of him. Titus had to get quite graphic before Tony came on board.

"I know you've decorated properties for him in this area," he said, "but have you been to any of his less attractive houses?"

Tony shook his head. "I've only done a couple for him and he bought them recently. They were very similar to this."

"He has places that are not fit to keep animals in Tony," said Titus. "And the people living there are crammed in, hot-bedding in most cases. They have had to give him their passports, if they had them, and they're working to get them back. Except they never do."

"What's hot-bedding?" I whispered to James.

"When people work in shifts they use the same bed," he whispered back. "When one gets up and goes to work, someone else sleeps in that bed. When they get up and go to work, someone else sleeps in it."

I pulled a face and shuddered.

"But that's by no means the worst of it," continued Titus. "Luan is part of an organisation that brings in drugs. It's a lucrative business but they need people to sell the drugs. Some of them are local but they bring people in too. And then they've branched out into using some of those people in other ways."

Sarah and Tony were sitting side by side and she was holding Tony's hand. They were leaning forward and listening intently. "Oh no," she whispered.

"He has a share in one of the clubs in Leeds. He calls it a night club but it's a contact place for sex workers really. That's his upmarket place compared to the others. He owns at least two houses here in town that are basically brothels," Titus continued, then paused looking at their faces.

"I know," said Sarah. "Well, suspected." Her voice was hardly more than a whisper. "I told Tony but we couldn't believe it. Is it really true?" She looked at Titus.

"I'm afraid so," he said. "But how did you know?"

"I work at the doctor's surgery in the town centre when I'm not on maternity leave," she said. "I'm an admin worker, so I have no direct contact with patients, but I know some of the girls have come in with medical problems, and there's been talk in the office. I wasn't sure if it was just speculation. We can't usually help them because they are not registered, not legally here. They come in hoping though, girls and boys. I once saw Luan picking one of them up outside."

"I'm afraid there's more," said Titus. "He's recently moved into pornography. It pays him very well I believe." That was something I had not thought of. There was a shocked silence as we absorbed this information.

Sarah looked up at the ceiling as we heard one of the children crying. We waited a few moments. The contrast between the innocent children upstairs and the plight of the people we were talking about was in all our minds as we listened. The crying stopped and we were all silent with our thoughts.

"That's where I come in," said James, after a few moments. "My mother didn't know any of this until yesterday, again it's all very secret, but part of my job is to try to find people who are involved in bad stuff on the internet. People that Luan must be dealing with, not just the users but the ones who are at the top of the chain, making the big money. My colleagues deal with sites on the dark web, these illegal sites where photographs and videos get passed on, but I mainly look for the financial links. Money laundering on a big scale gets most of the money out of the country to places where it's harder to trace. If I can get access to Luan's computer systems I could get a lot of information that would be really useful. We think Luan might also have paper documents that will provide information too. He's too self assured to take the precautions the bigger crooks do."

"And I'm working in his offices next week, where he's just set up all his new systems," said Tony. We all looked at him expectantly. Tony looked at Sarah and she nodded.

"Tell me what you need me to do," he said.

The three men spent the next hour planning how it would work. Tony was there for five nights so initially all that was necessary was to put in place some of the equipment that had been delivered to my house at James's request. There were bugs for telephones, some for light fittings and some fitted into covers that looked like plug sockets. They clipped over the actual sockets and couldn't be detected unless you knew what to look for. Tony would be working on his own so should have no trouble fitting them during the first night he was there. That should give lots of information to be going on with. If we needed access to the building, that would come later in the week.

We left with an agreement to keep each other up to date and meet again if necessary.

James was working from my house, with his boss's permission, until this job was done. Titus stayed too, so we were all together, to keep up to date with anything that was happening.

Chapter 11

It was midnight the next night when Titus got a call from Tony.

"It's all in place. I'm busy putting dust sheets out in the first office now. Luan met me here to let me in. The old guy who does security here won't bother about me. He's not interested really, just wants a quiet life. He spends his time looking at the screens occasionally but mostly planning his bets on the next day's races. He doesn't get up and walk round the building. Luan's office is on the third floor and he definitely can't be bothered to come up here. The cameras only cover the entrance and the corridors, not the offices themselves. Although the access to the service entrance is on camera so you might have to think about that."

"I've a bunch of keys for all Luan's offices including one he doesn't want me to decorate. It's his private office, he says, so that might be the one you want to look in. He obviously trusts me as he's just handed the whole bunch over. I didn't know at first whether to be flattered or guilty that he trusts me. In the end, I've decided just to be glad, because it gives us access to all his personal paperwork."

James sat down at his laptop and started checking that the bugs were working well. He and his colleagues back at base would hear everything that went on when Luan's office staff started work in the morning. We would just have to wait now to see if any information was forthcoming or if all they got was related to Luan's legitimate arms of his businesses. James said that even that was good information to have, as Luan could have partnerships or working arrangements with others from the shady side of business, eager to get involved in legitimate dealings. Any information was useful, but of course, the possibility of getting nitty gritty details from the personal office was exciting.

Thirty six hours later we were all back at Tony and Sarah's house discussing the next move forward. The conversations we had overheard via the bugs were virtually useless.

"Isn't there anything useful at all?" I asked James.

"I know where all the staff go to drink after work and where to get a smoke if I wanted to." I assumed he didn't mean buying cigarettes. "I know the girls all think Danny is hot, Harry is a geek, Helen is stuck up and Mia is your best bet for a good night out but don't take her home to meet your mother."

I gave him a hard stare.

"No, Ma, nothing useful as far as we're concerned. Everything dealt with in the outer offices is kosher business. We need access to Luan's inner sanctum and his computer and paperwork."

"Once we're in the office there's no problem," said James. "A, we won't be on camera, B, I can work my magic on the computer and C, Tony has had a quick look and there's lots of the old style paperwork in there. It didn't mean a lot to him but if we can take copies of anything interesting, I can look at it later and can see what's useful to send on to base. Luan keeps it locked away for a reason so there must be something dodgy about it. But we need a way to get in there without the security guard noticing. He may be the world's worst security guard but even he would raise the alarm if he saw two men walking into the building or down the corridors. We can't risk that," said James.

"Two men and a woman," I interrupted, putting down a tray of coffees that Sarah and I had made. "I said I wanted to do this with you and so far all I've done is the catering. I'm coming in too."

"That's not our only problem." It was Tony talking. He was in his paint splattered overalls ready to go out shortly. "Luan turned up at eleven o'clock the last two nights and he's said he will pop in tonight. That's fine, if there will just be me there working as he expects. But we have to be sure that he will not turn up when you are all there doing your stuff."

"We need a distraction," said Titus. "Something that will keep him out of the way while we poke about."

"We need two distractions," said James. "I need to get into the security office so I can turn off the cameras and destroy any chance of evidence that we have been in the building."

We were all quiet for a few minutes, sipping our drinks and deep in thought.

Then Sarah spoke. "Basically," she said, " we need to distract two men. What's the surest thing to get a man's attention apart from a football match on TV?"

She met my eyes.

"Give me a few hours," I said. "I've got the beginnings of an idea, but I need to talk to some friends."

We agreed to meet the following day, when we had made our plans.

****

It was early the following evening when Pat, Sandra, Trudy and I were in my sitting room.

"So spill the beans, girl," said Sandra, ever the practical one, wanting to get down to business. "What's the mystery?"

I had gathered everyone together without telling them why. All I had said was I had an urgent problem and needed their help. Good friends that they are, they had come over ready to help in whatever way they could.

I put down the tray of coffee cups I was bringing in from the kitchen and everyone helped themselves.

"It's quite complicated and a big ask," I started, "and not something you will ever be asked to do again."

Three faces were turned towards me waiting expectantly.

"You know how we keep saying that we are no use to anyone anymore, or not needed at least. Definitely not noticed."

This was hard to explain, I didn't want to offend anyone, or frighten them, but I wanted to tell them honestly that this had an element of danger in it.

"Here's our chance to prove that we are not on the scrap heap."

I looked round at all of them.

"There are things happening in this town that none of us know about." I paused and everyone waited expectantly.

"Things I've only learned about recently and that I thought only happened in films, or maybe in London and big cities. Bad things."

I had their attention.

"You know I've got quite friendly with Tony and Sarah?" They all nodded and waited again. "Well Tony's landlord is a man called Luan. My friend Titus knows a lot about him and he's not the sort of man you want to deal with. Tony has known him for years and thought he was a friend, but it turns out some of his business dealings are pretty shady. In fact, very shady. In fact, he's involved in drugs, and prostitution here in the town."

I waited a moment to see what response this produced.

Trudy was the first to speak.

"We're not totally innocent old ladies, you know Lizzie. We know there is stuff going on. There is enough in the papers, even the local ones, about people being caught growing marijuana, or smoking wacky backy. I've seen people passing pills in pubs and clubs myself."

"Really?!" said Pat.

"It's a bit more than that, Trudy," I said. "Luan and his associates are in this for big money. They are selling hard drugs and using forced labour to do it, and in their other businesses. They're even bringing people into the country illegally, getting them to sell drugs but also work in …" I hesitated, not sure how explicit to be. "…other ways. They don't usually have passports but if they do, Luan and his men take them. They're trapped. They can never escape the lifestyle."

Again I paused. I knew this was going to upset all the women. Pat in particular would find it hard to deal with.

"They run brothels, here in this little town, and elsewhere. And the people who work in them are not there by choice. They think they're coming here to be nannies, or work in beauty spas. And sometimes they are forced into pornography. They use these people in photographs, or make videos, really hard stuff, not just a bit of fun. It's really sick." I paused again.

"And the worst thing is, some of these people are kids."

There was silence for quite a while as everyone digested this information. Then Pat spoke. She was close to tears.

"How do you know this, Lizzie? How has Tony found out about it all? He's not involved is he?"

"Oh no. Maybe I didn't explain properly. It's actually Titus who has found out. He has connections from his time as a news reporter. They asked him to keep his eyes and ears open and share any information he found out. When he met Tony and learned of his connection with Luan, he told Tony to stay away from any dodgy dealings. Tony was as shocked as any of us."

They asked lots of questions. There was disbelief at first that what I was saying could be true, but I assured them there was no way this was a mistake. Of course, I couldn't tell them the full truth about Titus and James, their true roles in all this. We had decided that we would tell them that they were just acting as concerned citizens with good connections. We had to hope that the girls were naive enough to believe us.

Finding out that your hometown has an underworld you were not aware of takes a bit of time to register. I went to make more coffee while they took it all in and talked things over. When I came back they were ready to move on.

"So where do we come in?" said Sandra. Again the practical one.

I picked up my coffee mug.

"Titus believes that there is some information that would lead to the bad men higher up the chain and that it is in Luan's office. Now, it just so happens that he has asked Tony to decorate this office. Some of the information is on computers. Well, it would be these days, wouldn't it? This is where James can help. You know he is home for a few days. He's said that he would be prepared to help and you know he's a whizz on computers. There's some paperwork too that Titus would like to see."

"Is Tony able to get hold of this, take copies and stuff?" This was Sandra, asking the obvious.

"He can access it, but there is such a lot of it. And don't forget, he's already busy doing the decorating job. He can't spend hours looking through files. Plus he's not familiar with that sort of document. He might not know what's important."

"And the stuff on the computer will be password protected. James needs to get in himself, then he can access the information. We think there's lots of paperwork in the filing cabinet, more than one person can look through. Titus and I could look through that, take copies on our phones of anything that might be interesting. Then it can all be passed on to people that Titus and James know who will know what to do with it."

"Wow!" said Sandra, "This is pretty heavy stuff. You hear about these things on the TV but never think they actually happen somewhere you know."

"But this is our chance to make a difference," I said, "if you're up for it. I know it's a big ask."

"Of course we're up for it!" said Sandra. "Wouldn't miss it for the world."

"Hm," said Trudy, chuckling. "Not so much girl power as old girl power."

"To be fair, Trudy, it's your femme fatale capabilities we need from you." She grinned and shimmied her shoulders. "Sounds like it's a job just made for me. Tell me the details."

I told her about the need to distract the security guard who was on night duty in the swanky new office block in Leeds.

"James needs to get in to work on the security cameras first, then, when they're disabled, we can get into the specific offices we need to search."

"Who is this man? Give me some gen."

I could only tell her basic details.

"He's around sixty five years old, a bit of a gambler, especially on the horses, likes his beer and quite a letch but not with much going for him in the looks department."

"I know the type," said Trudy. "Not someone I'd go for usually, but it shouldn't be hard to keep his attention. Just give me the place and the time. It'll be a piece of cake."

"That's not what you need from me, I hope!" squeaked Pat, already beginning to panic.

"No love," I said, "I just need you to be pathetic."

Pat looked offended and I quickly corrected myself.

"Sorry pet, no, that's the wrong word. Vulnerable. I need you to be vulnerable, needing to be looked after. You can do that can't you?"

Pat preened herself.

"Well, yes, I can do my best."

"But what about me?" asked Sandra. "I can't see what you need me to do." She looked questioningly at me.

"Does your niece still work at Leeds Theatre?" I asked.

"Yes, she's the manager."

"We'll need some help from her if possible, but it might be best not to tell her the real reason why. I'll talk to you in a minute about that. But mainly we'll also need a driver, someone to pick people up in a hurry if things go wrong, someone who knows their way around the area but who can hide in the shadows and keep an eye on what's going on. Someone to keep in touch with the rest of the team, so we all know what's happening. This is one time when we really do want you to be invisible."

"I can do that. I wasn't a taxi driver for twenty years for nothing. Nobody notices taxi drivers." Sandra was her reliable self.

"So there's just Luan to keep out of the way," I said. "He has a habit of popping in on Tony to see how the work is going. We have to keep him occupied."

"How are you going to do that?"

There was a knock at the kitchen door and I left the room to answer it. A young blond woman was standing there.

"Good timing," I said. "Come on through and meet the girls."

We walked into the sitting room and three curious faces turned towards us.

"Meet Sarah," I said. "She's going to be our star performer."

Sarah and I had come up with this plan between us. The men were a bit reluctant to let us women get involved at first, very macho, believing they should be the only ones to take risks. After realising that they had no alternative plan, they had agreed.

I left Sarah getting to know the others while I went to make her a drink, but Trudy followed me through to the kitchen.

"Come on now, Lizzie. Spill the beans. There's more to this than you're telling us, honey, isn't there?"

I was running water into the kettle.

"What do you mean?"

"Come on, girl. Bit of a coincidence that James just happens to be here and you happened to get to know Titus, who has 'contacts' and has information that no-one else can get about what's going on in this town."

I put the switch down on the kettle and kept my back to her when I answered.

"Well, it is a coincidence. I couldn't believe it either at first."

"Ok, well let's say I accept that all of you meeting was a coincidence. Who are these contacts James and Titus have? What exactly does James do in London? They can't pass information like this to just anybody. They know people, don't they?"

I had turned round to face her now and was surprised how intensely she was looking at me. She wasn't going to be put off.

"Look, there are things I can't tell you."

"Or you'll have to kill me?"

"Not me, Trudy, but maybe somebody would."

We stared at each other. I was holding my breath. Suddenly, Trudy seemed to make a decision.

"Fair enough," she said. "Better get that coffee through to Sarah and we can find out what exactly you have planned."

I took a deep breath and let it out slowly. I made Sarah's coffee and we went back to join the others.

****

It took us another hour or so to work out the details. We were just going through it for one more time when Titus, Tony and James arrived. They had been to the village pub while we got our act together and, if I'm honest, to give them some male bonding time. Tony was struggling with Sarah's role in our plan. He needed to talk to Titus and James to develop some insight into their characters, to develop a trust in their judgement. Happy hour, six to seven at our pub on Thursday nights, was pretty quiet, even given the cheap drinks, and there were plenty of quiet corners where they could huddle together and talk privately. Hopefully that's what had happened.

"Everything sorted?" James asked, as he hugged me when they came in.

Tony went to sit next to Sarah. "I can't say I'm happy about this, but these guys have convinced me we have to do it." Sarah smiled at him.

"You'd better get your working togs on, love," she said. "There's another night's decorating for you now, while we finish up here. We don't want to alert Luan by changing your routine at the last minute."

Tony made his way to the door to collect his bag of work clothes from the hall and take them to the bathroom and change. When he came downstairs again, Sarah went into the hall to say goodbye to him, then returned.

"I'm putting everyone on a group WhatsApp chat," said James. "We all need to keep in touch tomorrow and this is the simplest way. Put your phones on silent tomorrow night. We don't want ringtones giving us away in the middle of things."

"I don't think I can do WhatsApp," said Pat. "What does it do?"

"Let me look at your phone," said Trudy. She held out her hand. "Gosh, Pat, this thing is out of the ark."

James held his hand out and took the phone. "Mmm. Maybe we don't need you on the group chat too, Pat. You will be with Sarah or Sandra all the time, so they can keep you up to speed. Keep your phone with you though, just in case we need another way of keeping in touch, and make sure it's charged before you go out tomorrow. That goes for everyone else too."

There were more details to put in place, phone calls to make, but the plan was going to go ahead.

Chapter 12

The following evening, Sarah was in the bathroom putting finishing touches to her makeup. Her husband was leaning in the doorway watching her. He was dressed ready for work. Sarah was wearing a sleeveless halter-necked red top in a silky material, with a tight band under her bust. Her back was bare from the halter neck to her waist and the outfit was completed by matching wide legged trousers and black high heels. As she leaned forward to see her face better in the mirror the trousers stretched tighter over her rear. Tony admired the view for a moment, then snapped to attention.

"I'm not happy about this," he said

"We've been through this before." She put her mascara away and turned to push past him. "What's the best way to distract a man's attention from his job?"

"You're certainly distracting me from mine." He turned and followed her down the stairs.

"I'll be fine. I won't be on my own, remember. You'd better go now. My taxi is due soon." Tony reluctantly kissed her cheek and opened the front door.

"Just be careful." He gave her one last look and left.

Sarah went into the sitting room, picked up a small black bag and popped her mobile phone in it, then draped a black pashmina round her shoulders.

"You're a bit OTT for a night out with the girls aren't you?" her mother said, dangling Samuel on her knee.

"That's what Tony thinks Mum, but it's the first night out I've had in ages. Let me enjoy myself. And thanks again for looking after the children."

"You look really pretty Mummy," said Jacob, coming to kiss her.

"Thank you darling." She bent to give him a hug. "I fed Samuel less than an hour ago, Mum. There's a bottle of expressed milk in the fridge. You know what to do with it, don't you?"

"We'll be fine, love. You have a good time."

"I don't know what time I will be back, and Tony could be out all night too so you go to bed. Don't wait up for me." Sarah kissed her mum just as a car tooted outside. "That will be the taxi," she said, "better go," and she blew the children kisses as she left.

She had plenty of time to think as the taxi drove to Leeds. She hoped she could carry this off. She felt strangely vulnerable in the borrowed outfit, it was not her usual style at all. She was tempted to hunch her shoulders and try to hide the figure hugging effect of the top. She had initially taken some convincing that she had her post pregnancy figure back sufficiently to wear it. Tony's reaction when she tried it on to show him convinced her it was right for the job. He thought she looked fabulous. He just didn't want her to wear it for anyone else.

As the taxi pulled up outside the theatre she pressed to send a message on her phone, then dropped it into her bag again.

She pulled her shoulders back and put a smile on her face as Luan bent to open the door for her. He held out his hand to help her out of the cab.

She looked up at him and reached forward to give him a peck on his cheek, letting the pashmina fall from one shoulder as she did so. "This is so kind of you," she breathed into his ear. "I can't remember the last time anyone gave me such a wonderful treat."

"My pleasure." Luan's eyes were wide and his usually cynical expression was replaced by a surprised smile. He really couldn't believe his luck. He knew Sarah was attractive but she looked stunning tonight. And she had always seemed to avoid his company before. When she phoned to suggest taking him up on his offer of a night out he had been amazed, but then when she had suggested tonight, because Tony would be working he began to understand. She wanted to have a bit of fun without her husband knowing about it. Well, he could arrange that easily enough. He could find Tony plenty of other night work to keep him out of the way.

It had been a bit of a hassle getting tickets for tonight's show at such short notice. He had strings he could pull in most places, but he'd not mixed in these circles before. It had taken a bit of effort but eventually he had found someone he could put pressure on to give up tickets in exchange for cash. He was sure Sarah would be worth it.

"Shall we go into the bar?" he said, threading her arm through his. "I think we have plenty of time for a drink before the show starts."

In the city centre another phone vibrated as Sarah's text arrived.

'Pulling up at the theatre now.' The same message went to Tony's phone and the rest of the team.

The first recipient put her phone in her bag then drove a short distance to the front of a huge, glass fronted office block. She stopped for a while, pretending to look at her satnav in case she was being watched, then sent a message of her own. "I'm going in now," it said.

She climbed out of the car and went to the wide front doors. She tried the handles but, as expected, they were locked. Peering through the glass she banged loudly.

Inside the building the security guard looked up from his mobile phone. He scanned the screens in front of him and clicked on the image showing the front doors to enlarge the picture. His night shift peace had only ever been disturbed once before, on his previous job, and then it was a smartly clad young man who worked in the building who had left some paperwork behind. There had been a bit of a delay while he checked the man's security tags, but then he had been in and out in a few seconds.

This time the camera showed a slim, older woman in tight, white jeans, high heels and a close fitting cowl necked top. He guessed she was in her mid sixties, but very attractive. A bit of a Joan Collins type or maybe Joanna Lumley. Yes, definitely Joanna Lumley. He had a bit of a thing for Joanna Lumley. The woman was banging on the door again now and looking through the glass doors into the dimly lit interior.

He wasn't supposed to open the doors to anyone, of course, but what the hell. Who would know anyway, nobody ever checked the damned recordings and what kind of a risk was she anyway? He picked up his keys and walked out of his office into the foyer.

"What's the problem, love?" he said as he opened the door. The woman pushed past him and into the building. She really was rather attractive, just his type.

"Oh, you are a life-saver, you lovely man," she said, wriggling provocatively. "Where are the loos? I'm absolutely desperate."

He pointed to a corridor to the right and she hurried off.

A few minutes later she was back, beaming and raising her eyes to heaven.

"So sorry," she gushed, "I didn't know where to go. You are an absolute darling," and she gave him a kiss on his cheek. "I've been driving around for hours, totally lost." She was holding his hand and looking into his eyes. "Can't believe how long I've been. I was supposed to go to a party and I think I've got the wrong post code." She stopped to draw breath. "Sorry, my name's Trudy," she said.

"Geoff," he said, then let his mouth drop open again. His tongue wasn't actually hanging out, but close to it.

"So are you in charge here then?" She looked around. "Where's your den? Can I see your equipment?" She giggled suggestively and put a hand on his chest. "I do love a man in uniform," she said.

A few minutes later they were sitting side by side in the security office, holding mugs of the wine she had brought in her bag that was supposedly for the party. "I don't think I'm going to get to this party, you know. We may as well have this now," she had said. Geoff had not taken any persuading.

Now they were both looking at the screens.

"Do you work all this stuff then, you clever man?" Trudy asked. "What does it do?

"You can see what's happening in any part of the building," said Geoff proudly, pressing buttons and scrolling to demonstrate. He enlarged pictures of some areas, and showed the exterior of the back door, where she could see Tony's van was parked.

"Like this?" Trudy asked, pressing two or three buttons in quick succession.

"Careful, not too fast!" Geoff put his hand out to stop her and she moved back quickly, causing some of her wine to slop over the side of the keyboard..

"Bugger!" he said, jumping up and pulling a rather grubby handkerchief out of his trouser pocket. "Bugger!" He mopped the keyboard carefully.

"Oh dear! I hope I haven't caused you a problem," Trudy looked apologetic.

"No, I think it's alright" Geoff was still mopping, now using his equally grubby tea towel.

"Perhaps I'd better go," Trudy stood up. She took her phone out of her bag and pretended to ring a number from her speed dial as he continued to mop. After a brief conversation she had apparently got the correct postcode from her friend. "Silly me," she told Geoff. "I thought it was E45, like the cream, but it's E54."

Geoff had calmed down now. There didn't seem to be any damage done so no danger of the bosses finding out what he was up to. "Don't rush off," he said. "Finish your wine and leave me your phone number before you go at least." He patted the seat next to him and Trudy sat down.

Fifteen minutes later he had put the phone number she had given him into his phone and they were deep into a discussion about which pub they could meet in when there was a loud knocking at the door. Twice in one night. Geoff couldn't believe it.

This time there was a young man at the door, dressed in jeans and casual jacket and with a laptop case hanging from a strap across his body. As Geoff got to the glass doors the man held up a security pass on a lanyard around his neck. It bore his photo and the logo of Citywide Security Equipment Ltd. along with a number. Geoff opened the door.

"You had some damage to the equipment, mate?" said the man, pushing the door further open and coming in.

"Don't think so," said Geoff, following him into the office.

"Hello, hello, hello! Who's this then?"

Trudy had stood up and was looking sheepish. The young man looked at the bottle of wine as she topped up her cup, then at Geoff.

"It's not what it looks like," said Geoff, panicking but not sure what to say next.

"Not my problem mate," said the young man. "All I know is, I'm on my way to another call and I get told to do an emergency detour to your place. Head office have noticed something wrong with the system in the last few minutes. You've got a five star contract which means it's connected to head office all the time. If there's a fault they spot it straight away and they have to sort it out quickly. I just happened to be passing. It's your lucky night." He had put down his bag on the chair and was opening it up. He glanced at Trudy then back to Geoff.

"In more ways than one by the looks of it."

"I really had better go," said Trudy, picking up her things. "I hope I haven't caused you any trouble."

This time, Geoff didn't try to stop her. He picked up his keys again and walked with her to the door. "I'll phone you and we can fix up a date," he said hopefully.

She nodded and looked back at the open office door where the young man was busy at work. "See you," and she hurried to her car, fiddled with her satnav, presumably putting the correct postcode into it, then drove off, waving to him as he locked the doors again.

The young man, who said his name was Jim, accepted Geoff's offer of a cup of tea while he worked.

"Am I going to be in bother about any of this?" Geoff asked him.

"Not from me mate," said Jim. "Looks like you might have spilled a drop of liquid on the keyboard. Happens all the time. I'll have it fixed in a jiffy and upgrade your system while I'm at it. With a five star contract you're due a service call anytime now anyway. No need to mention anything to anyone as far as I'm concerned."

"Thanks," said Geoff, putting the mug of tea carefully on the desk, then turning back to the sink. He poured the rest of the wine from the bottle and the mugs down the plughole and flushed it away. Best not to take any more chances tonight.

Twenty minutes later James left the building, supposedly going back to his car. Instead he walked round the office block, talking on his phone as he walked.

"It's all done Tony. Geoff, bless him, is happily watching a recording of the security footage from last night on his screens. Plus I've planted a gismo on the equipment so our guys at base can track who comes and goes in the building from now on." He chuckled. "Hopefully, they're less easily distracted than our Geoff. I've called Titus and he and Mum are walking over from her car to meet me now, so you can come down and open the service door to let us in whenever you're ready."

Chapter 13

Sarah was struggling to concentrate on the show. It was a musical, her favourite, and a production that was getting rave revues, but her proximity to Luan made her uncomfortable. He'd made no moves as yet, but now she knew the sort of thing he was involved in, sitting near to him made her flesh creep. He smelled of cigarette smoke, which she hated, and a very strong aftershave that she would never smell again without thinking of him. At least she had made it to the interval without a problem.

They made their way down the stairs to collect the interval drinks Luan had ordered for them and she managed to make small talk about the show. Theatre was not really Luan's thing but this show was about gangsters, which was interesting. The principal characters were all women, which was not so interesting, though they were very skimpily dressed, which he liked. He tried to show interest to please her. Then he got a ping on his phone.

"Sorry," he apologised. "It is business. I have to take this." She smiled and nodded.

"I'd better check in on Mum and the kids anyway."

He walked a few paces from the bar and turned away from her with the phone to his ear.

Sarah pulled her own phone out of her bag and quickly typed a message. "Everything ok?" We're just at the interval here."

A few seconds later her phone vibrated with a reply. "All going as planned. No worries." She quickly deleted the messages as Luan returned, in case he could see her phone.

"Everything okay?" she asked, forcing a smile she hoped was natural.

"Nothing I can't handle," he said, putting his hand around her waist and standing much closer than she felt comfortable with. "I have many businesses and sometimes there are things to be done that only the boss can do." He smiled, sure he was impressing her. He picked up his glass of wine and drank it down as the auditorium bell rang.

"Time to go back to our seats," Sarah said, thankfully.

They walked up the stairs and shuffled along the row to their places. Three rows behind them, two women were watching their movements carefully. As Sarah turned to push her flip seat down she looked up at them and nodded slightly.

Getting those seats had not been easy. Luckily, Sandra had come up trumps. Her niece, the theatre manager, had proved helpful. Sandra had spun her a story about Luan, a mature man of the world, taking out Sarah who she had described as being Pat's granddaughter, young and innocent. Sandra and Pat wanted to keep an eye on them.

The manager had recently had some trouble herself. Her daughter had run away with an older man from her office, much to the family's distress. She was eager to help someone else avoid a similar situation. She always had a number of seats for emergencies, in case a local celebrity arrived unexpectedly, or someone made a huge fuss about their seats being unsuitable. They could be moved to spare seats rather than disturb the whole audience, or even the show.

In this case, she had persuaded a couple that they had been upgraded to seats in a box, leaving the seats they had booked, three rows behind Luan and Sarah, for Sandra and Pat. The couple were delighted, feeling like royalty in the box, even though the view from there was not nearly as good as from the seats they had given up. But it was their twenty fifth wedding anniversary. The wife was convinced her husband had arranged it all as a surprise for her, and he was happy to let her think it.

****

Back in the office block, Tony made his way down the corridors carrying a large bundle of dust sheets. Just on the off chance that Geoff was walking the building, unlikely but possible, he could say he had come to shake them out at the back of the building, using the service door. As expected, there was no sign of the security guard and Tony was able to let his three friends in without being spotted.

"All quiet on the western front?" said James in a whisper as he walked inside. Despite his apparent bravado he wanted this operation to go as smoothly as possible, not least because I was with him. He and Titus had tried to talk me out of tagging along, but I had been adamant. We'd had quite a long conversation about it.

"As far as I am concerned this is all I am contributing to the investigation, no matter what you say about my organisational skills, or ability to bring you all together. I need to be part of the action."

"You're a facilitator Lizzie," Titus had said. "You made the plan and you are the link that joined us all together. This wouldn't be happening without you."

"No! No more holding the coats. You're all taking risks," I had argued. "If my planning is flawed I couldn't live with myself if you got caught and I wasn't even there. I'll be fine."

Now I was actually here I was a little less confident. We were walking up the stairs to the third floor, so conversation had to stop for a while. I needed all my breath for climbing. I really hoped there would be no running involved tonight. I was wearing my joggers and trainers, but even so, sprinting had never been my forte.

Luan's suite of offices consisted of several individual rooms, each visible through glass walls. As we walked through we could see there were dust sheets, brushes, paint pots and so on in one of them, where Tony had worked that night so far.

"Do you have much left to do in there?" Titus asked Tony, as we walked past.

"I'll need a couple of hours but that should be all," he said. "Luan has come to check how it's going at about eleven o'clock each night this week but, of course, that should be different tonight."

"What's the latest? Have you heard anything recently?"

"Not since we had that message from Sarah a few minutes ago when the first half had just finished. The show's due to finish soon after 10pm."

"That probably won't be long enough, but we knew that. Let's hope the girls are able to put plan B into operation."

We had reached an office that had blanked off windows now. Tony opened the door and we all trooped in. There was a desk, with a laptop, side cupboards, a printer, a filing cabinet and the usual contents of an office. Photographs on the wall were of Luan shaking hands with local councillors, presenting prizes to a team of young footballers, all the sorts of things that portrayed him as a benevolent business man.

"Better get to work then," said James, putting his bag on the chair in front of the desk and taking out his laptop and various cables. "Titus, you and Mum see what you can find in the filing cabinet, it might take a while to get through that paperwork. Once I've copied this stuff I can look at whatever is on it later but you've only got the time that we can stay here."

"I'll get back to the decorating and leave you to it then," said Tony. "Let me know if you hear anything from Sandra or Sarah, just in case I miss it"

A while later, James had been working on Luan's computer for some time. Titus and I were searching through desk drawers and files. Titus had taken lots of photographs of documents that he thought might be important and some that definitely were. We were all quiet except for the odd question from me as I showed Titus a document I thought might be useful.

Tony had finished his work and packed up all his stuff ready to take it out to his van, but was deliberately waiting to do that till everyone else had left. He kept looking at his phone, hoping to get another message from Sarah, but nothing so far. They had looked up the estimated time for the show to finish so he knew that it would end in a few minutes.

"The show will be over soon," he said. "Are we going to be done?" He was hoping so, but didn't really expect that it would be the case.

"There's a lot of stuff here," said Titus, taking another picture. "We're going to need more time. We talked about this Tony." He paused and looked across the room at Tony.

"Sarah knows what to do. She's a clever girl and she won't take risks. Remember, she won't be on her own."

Tony sighed. "Yeah, I know," he said. "Ok, I'll tell them to go for plan B," and he sent a message.

****

The lights went on in the auditorium and everyone started to make their way to the exits. Sarah felt her phone vibrate and managed to take a quick look at the screen as she side-stepped between the seats following Luan. "Plan B." She took a deep breath. So be it. If they needed more time they should have it.

Behind her, another phone had vibrated with the same message. Two elderly ladies pushed their way along the seats. They fell into step behind Luan and Sarah, shuffling along as the crowd walked down the corridor to the staircase.

As they reached the last few stairs, with Luan's hand uncomfortably warm on the small of Sarah's back, she caught sight of the elderly woman to her left. At the last couple of steps, the woman stumbled, as if pushed from behind and grabbed Sarah's arm to stop herself falling. Sarah held on to her as the woman's legs crumpled.

"Oh! Oh my ankle!" cried the woman, as a couple at her other side also held on to her to stop her falling.

"Auntie Pat!" said Sarah. "Are you alright?!"

The crowds were clearing a little and Sarah moved Pat to the side slightly, Pat hopping and not putting her weight on her left foot.

"I've twisted my ankle," said Pat. "Someone pushed me from behind."

Luan was standing beside them, looking a bit impatient. Sarah explained.

"This is my aunt, Pat. Pat, this is a friend of mine and Tony's, Luan." Luan nodded reluctantly.

"I didn't know you were here Auntie Pat," said Sarah. "Surely you've not come on your own."

"Oh no, I came with Sandra, but she hurried off to get her bus. Then someone pushed me from behind. I'm not as steady on my feet as I used to be. I nearly ended up on the floor!"

"Come over here," said Sarah, trying to manoeuvre Pat into a corner where there was space. "Let's get you out of the way of all these people. Does your ankle hurt?"

Pat tried to hobble a few steps but almost fell as she put her weight on the injured ankle. She grabbed Luan's arm this time and put most of her weight on him.

"Oh, I feel dizzy! I think I might be going to faint," she said.

"Luan, can you find her a chair?" said Sarah.

"I think I'm going to be sick," said Pat.

Luan quickly hurried off to find a chair, leaving Sarah to deal with her aunt. Round the corner, Sandra watched from behind a pillar.

Luan returned with a chair and they settled Pat on it, her left leg pointedly out in front of her.

"Your ankle does look really swollen already," said Sarah, kneeling in front of her. Pat quickly pushed her other leg further out of sight, under the chair and spread her skirt out to hide it. Her right leg was even more swollen than the left actually. They always were by this time of night. Sarah examined the ankle then looked up at Pat.

"Do you feel better now?" She turned round to look up into Luan's face.

"Do you think you could get her a glass of water Luan?" Luan's expression showed his reluctance but he walked towards the bar area.

Sarah managed to give Sandra a brief nod while his back was turned, then squeezed Pat's hand.

"You were brilliant, Pat. I actually thought you were going to fall."

"I nearly did!" said Pat. "I really did get pushed by someone, and I think I know who," and she glared at the pillar where Sandra was still lurking.

"Are you okay?" Sarah gave her a good look. "You are a bit pale actually."

Luan arrived with the water and handed it to Pat who took a grateful sip.

"Luan I don't like the look of this ankle," said Sarah. "I think we need to get it checked, she might have broken it. I'm going to phone for an ambulance."

Luan looked appalled. This was not how he had planned the rest of the evening. He had intended to hail a taxi outside the theatre and was hoping to persuade Sarah to go back to his new apartment. If not, at least he would try to get her to agree to a drink in a bar and maybe something to eat. Then she might change her mind, after a few glasses of wine.

"Keep an eye on Pat for a minute please, while I find somewhere quiet to make the phone call." Sarah walked to the other side of the pillar, near Sandra, where Luan couldn't hear her conversation. He stood glowering at Pat as she sipped her water saying "Oh dear," or sighing dramatically.

"Hello Tony, everything is going ahead for plan B here." She knew that would be his first concern. "I'm just pretending to phone for an ambulance for Pat. How are things going at the offices?" She gave Sandra a quick nod then turned back to watch Luan as he stood awkwardly beside Pat.

Five minutes later she was back beside them, having had a brief conversation with Tony.

"It's hopeless, Luan," she said. "The state of the NHS is frightening. They say they can't get an ambulance out for at least two hours. It might be even more if other more urgent calls come in as the night goes on. Apparently, an elderly woman with a suspected broken ankle is not a priority!"

Pat whimpered with presumed pain and heaved heavy sighs. Sarah put her hands on Luan's arm and looked into his eyes.

"We can't wait for the ambulance, and we can't leave her here," she said. "Do you think you could possibly get a taxi and we can take her to the hospital?"

Luan's face showed his horror. His evening was now looking very different to the one he had planned.

"Hospital!" he said. He had a phobia about hospitals. "No, I cannot go there!"

"Oh please, Luan." Sarah slipped her left hand up to his shoulder and leaned into him so that she was pressed against his chest. It was almost five hours now since she had fed Samuel and her breasts were swollen and stretching the silky fabric of her top. Luan looked down and she reached her right arm across his body, pulling him towards her slightly. "I know you won't leave her like this," and she looked up at him with wide blue eyes.

A few minutes later, Sandra watched as Luan and Sarah helped Pat across the foyer of the theatre, over the pavement and into the waiting taxi. Once Pat was settled in her seat and the door closed, Sarah hurried round to get in the cab from the other side and Luan sat in front, next to the driver. As they drove away, Sandra came out of the shadows and phoned Lizzie.

"All going well so far," she said. "I'm walking back to my car now and I'll drive to the hospital. I'll let you know what happens there. How are things going at the office?"

"So far so good," I said. "Trudy did a brilliant job. I'll let her know to head for A & E now and you two can keep an eye on Sarah and Pat together. Keep us in the loop but it doesn't look as if Luan is going to ditch them yet anyway. We might have at least another hour before we need to pack up."

Sandra chuckled. "His eyes are out on stalks whenever he looks at Sarah. She's got him wrapped round her little finger."

I smiled. "I'd better not tell Tony that. He's neurotic about her being with Luan anyway. Keep in touch, especially if anything changes"

"Everything alright?" said Tony, coming into the office as I put my phone back in my pocket.

"Plan B is well under way," I said. "Sandra will keep us updated, she's on her way to the hospital now to meet Trudy to watch what's happening."

"Well I've finished the job here so I can take all my stuff down to the service door ready to load it into my van then I'm ready to leave. But I'll come and give you a hand when I've done that."

Titus looked up from some papers he had spread over the side desk. He had his reading glasses on and looked over them at Tony.

"Yeah, I could do with your help here," he said. "Some of these are in Albanian and mine's a bit rusty to say the least."

"I'll be back as quick as I can," and Tony left.

Chapter 14

"How is it going with the laptop?" I asked James.

"Oh I've been in for a while. Just making sure I have everything copied. It takes a while to load. It's ridiculously unprotected considering how much information is on here. Luan's not careful about keeping his records private at all, and his contacts would have a fit if they realised how he's compromising them. I'm definitely going to get into tracing some big money and other stuff too."

"Good stuff?" Titus was looking across again.

"Some of it is very good. Bank accounts and financial dealings. They should provide a trail to other people with a bit of luck. I'll need a good look when I get them back home. Then there's some nasty stuff as well. Pornographic sites in particular. I'm not sure how much is Luan's personal taste and how much is what you might call sales samples."

"Oh James, that's awful." I looked up from the file I was sifting through.

"Sorry, Ma." He pulled a face at me. "It's pretty heavy stuff, some of the worst I've seen. Although it's not my area of expertise at all. I'll leave it for the specialists at base to see what they make of it. I'm more into finding viruses and keeping people safe, or following the money."

I smiled at him ruefully. I was pleased to hear that.

We carried on working for a while, Titus taking photographs occasionally, James tapping at the keyboard, and me looking through the files in the filing cabinet and pulling out anything I thought was interesting.

We could hear Tony moving about in the office next door but after a few minutes he appeared in our doorway.

"Right, I'm done now, everything is by the service door. What do you want me to look at Titus?" he said.

"I've put some papers on the desk here. It looks to me like they're moving something large around but I don't know exactly what. Can you make it out?"

Tony opened a file and started looking through the documents. Everyone worked quietly for a few minutes then I jumped as the phone in my pocket vibrated. It was Sandra calling.

"Hello, everything's ok. It's absolutely manic here in A & E. How's it going with you?"

"Ploughing on, there's lots to get through. Can you see Sarah and Pat?"

"Yes, they're still in the queue. There's so many people in front of them, they've not even been through triage yet. Pat's in a wheelchair and Sarah's got Luan pushing it. His face is a picture." I could tell she was smiling as she spoke. "Sarah sent him off to find the wheelchair when they arrived so I had a quick word while he was out of the way. They're both fine. Pat's not hurt at all but she's playing it really well."

"Where are you now? Can Luan see you and Trudy?"

"No chance. We're sort of round the corner and behind them. There's so many people here, he would never notice us anyway. We came straight in after I met Trudy. Nobody challenged us or asked us if we're okay. They just assume we're waiting for someone or for attention ourselves. There's a sign up saying that non-urgent cases will be seen as soon as possible but that it's likely to be a four hour wait."

"Do you think Luan can wait it out?" I said hopefully.

"Doubt it," said Sandra. "Looking at his face he's not a happy chappy. But Sarah's vamping him into submission." Tony looked across at me. I had the phone on speaker so we could all hear. "She's definitely the only reason he's still here."

"Well, let us know if anything changes and take care, all of you," I said, and shut the phone down.

Tony and I exchanged a look. This was really hard for him. Not only had he lost someone who he had thought of as a friend, he had found out he was one of the worst types of criminal. Moreover, his wife was in the company of this man and he couldn't protect her. Things could turn really nasty if Luan were to realise what Sarah and the rest of us were up to while she was still with him. Or even later, if we didn't find enough information to have Luan arrested, or the authorities didn't act quickly enough to get him and his henchmen in custody. Sarah and Tony would be the most at risk of any of us.

Titus and Tony examined a file together.

"What do you make of this?" Titus said. "It's obviously something coming into the country, being stored or moved on at different points in the journey. It gets handed over like any other delivery but I can't work out what it is. What does this word mean? I don't have the English translation for it, but it's on each of these sheets." He pointed to a specific word.

"Hmm, not exactly sure. Remember I left Kosovo when I was eight. We spoke Albanian at home, at least some of the time, but it was functional, family conversation. Not business language. The nearest I can guess is 'packages' or perhaps 'merchandise'."

"Whatever it is, they come in small numbers, look. This one says four, another one three, never more than five at a time."

"Yes," said Titus, "I've noticed that. "It can't be cigarettes or booze. You would have a van load of that sort of cargo. Not drugs either. I suppose it could just be a code word for something but what?"

"And it's only been coming in recently," said Tony, pointing to dates. "Usually stays overnight then moves on, further north, but always to big cities. No actual addresses, just contact phone numbers."

Titus was busy taking photographs of every page. He pulled one page forward to take a picture, then stopped and pointed to the date.

"Look at this one," he pushed it towards Tony. "That's today's date. Whatever it is, four pieces of this merchandise are coming today, then moving on to Newcastle tomorrow."

"Well, they won't bring them here. Deliveries don't come to offices anyway. They will go to his storage premises in Selford."

James stopped what he was doing and came over to look while I waited expectantly.

"What are you thinking?" I asked after they had been silent for a few moments.

"I am trying to think what could be so big that four could fill a van. All I can think of is armaments, but that would be completely out of Luan's business model so far." This was James talking. "Of course, it doesn't actually say what size the transport is, large van, small van. I suppose it could even be a car."

There was an almost audible intake of breath as we realised the implications of what that meant.

"Do you think these pieces of merchandise are actually people?" My mouth was hanging open again and I shut it quickly. This was a horrible thought but it did seem to tie in.

In the silence that followed my question, Tony's phone vibrated. He took it from his pocket and looked at it.

"It's Luan," he said.

****

At the hospital Luan was putting money into the drinks machine to get two teas for Sarah and Pat. He had dialled Tony's number while he was queueing for his turn, but Tony hadn't answered. Luan assumed he was up a ladder or something. He carried the drinks back to the two women.

"Thank you so much. This is so welcome," said Sarah, genuinely ready for a drink, even if it was stewed and strong from the machine. She handed on one of the paper cups to Pat who smiled weakly and took a grateful sip.

Luan took out his phone again.

"Excuse me," he said, "I have to make this call." He sat next to Sarah and put the phone to his ear.

"Tony, at last my friend. Were you knee deep in paint pots? You didn't answer when I rang a few minutes ago."

Sarah and Pat sat motionless, straining to hear above the noise of the busy A & E department. Tony's reply was indistinct and short.

"No worry my friend. Listen. I have some merchandise being delivered tonight and I need the keys to my lock up in Selford. Sami has the goods in his little blue van and the idiot has left his keys somewhere. He'll be with you anytime soon.

Let him have the bunch of keys you have and he can take off the ones he wants. He will call you when he gets to the service door and you can open it for him, no need to bother that idiot Geoff."

There was another indecipherable comment from Tony, then Luan continued.

"How is the job going? Will you be finished tonight as you thought?"

Again more indistinct chatter. "You can let me have the rest of the keys back when you finish then. Drop them at the security desk with Geoff before you leave and I will pick them up in the morning. You have the key to my private office on that bunch too. Can you find it?"

He was quiet again, presumably waiting for Tony to find the key, although Sarah suspected he might be in the office already, and certainly Lizzie and the other two men were.

"Ok my man. Go in and look in the right hand desk drawer." He waited till Tony said something else. "You found a brown envelope? That's it, that's for you. I pay you now, before I see the job, my friend. I know what a good job you do."

There was another pause as Tony talked to him again.

"Well, is a good job I'm sure. Better get off the phone now, in case Sami trying to get you. Chow, baby!"

Pat looked at Sarah wide eyed as Luan put his phone away. There was good news in the sense that Luan was not planning on dropping in on Tony at the office, but bad news that Sami was on his way. Sarah turned to Luan.

"Luan, Pat is in desperate need of the loo. Will you wait here while I take her? They might call her name while we're in there and we would miss her place in the queue."

Luan had accepted that his night had gone truly awry by now. He was resigned to the thought that this was a trust building exercise with Sarah. Convinced that she was really wanting to spend more time with him without Tony knowing, he felt sure that their next outing would be more to his taste. He nodded resignedly and took his phone out again as Sarah stood and began to push Pat's wheelchair to the back of the room where there was a sign indicating the disabled toilet further down the corridor.

Trudy spoke quietly to Sandra.

"Keep an eye on his nibs while I see if I can sneak a word with Sarah." She too walked to the back of the room. Once out of sight she was able to hurry to catch up with the other two women as they approached the disabled toilet.

"What's happening?" she hissed as she reached them.

"I need to call Lizzie and find out," said Sarah. "We've just heard Luan talking to Tony and telling him that Sami is on his way to the office. I'm going to phone her now." She pushed the wheelchair into the large cubicle and Trudy waited impatiently outside for what seemed ages. Eventually the pair came out, Pat looking sheepish and explaining that they had taken so long because she really had needed the toilet.

"Never mind all that," said Trudy impatiently, "what's going on?"

"I got through to Lizzie and she told me Tony was downstairs with Sami. He'd had the call from Luan that we overheard, then almost immediately Sami called to say he was at the service door of the office block. Apparently he needed keys for a lock up."

"Golly, so what happened, do you know?"

"It's ok, Tony came back upstairs while I was still on the phone to Lizzie. He had handed over the keys and Sami has gone to the lock up now. The trouble is, Titus thinks they should go after him to see what this important load is that Sami is putting in the lock up overnight."

"They have finished at the offices anyway, so Lizzie, Titus and James are discussing whether to hot foot it over there to have a look while Tony cleans up and leaves."

"Does that mean we can go home now?" asked Pat hopefully. "I am really tired. It's well past my bedtime."

"Try to hold out a bit longer Pat," said Sarah. "We don't want Luan running off to check the lock up too. Let's try to give them as much time as we can."

They let Trudy leave first, sliding back into her seat to bring Sandra up to speed with the latest news. Sarah pushed the wheelchair back to the end of the row and sat down next to Luan.

"Did we miss anything while we were at the toilet?" she asked him.

"More druggies and scum come through the door every minute and a man rushed in with his hand bandaged up, bleeding all over the place so they rushed him through to the back."

Sarah looked at Luan in surprise.

"I mean, has anybody called Pat yet?"

"Oh, yeah, no. I mean, no. Nobody called her." He had actually lost interest and not listened, so he realised it was possible he had missed Pat's name being called. "Maybe she got missed off the list. Maybe I should go and check at the desk." He started to get up from his seat.

"No, it's okay," Sarah stood up quickly and put her hand on his arm. "It had better be me that goes, because I booked her in. I'll check what's happening."

She moved off to stand at the reception desk, aware that they had been waiting several hours now. It was likely that they would be calling Pat's name soon if it had not already been called. She was not an urgent case, but an elderly lady with a suspected broken bone would surely be seen soon. They could go through the motions of getting Pat checked but they would be dismissed as soon as anyone looked at her leg.

She stood at the desk waiting patiently, in no hurry to push to the front and keeping an eye on Luan who was on his phone again. Eventually she was told that Pat would be seen 'soon'. No surprise there, then. She walked back to her seat.

Luan was having an animated conversation on his phone in Albanian. Something was obviously wrong. She hoped it was nothing to do with Tony or the others and sat waiting agitatedly. Trying to distract herself she looked round the waiting area and noticed a couple with a baby sitting a few rows in front of them. The baby was crying and the young mother took a bottle from a bag at her feet. Sarah immediately thought about Samuel. She felt her breasts tingle. It was more than seven hours since she had fed him and she was feeling swollen and uncomfortable.

At that moment Luan finished his call abruptly. "Is everything alright?" Sarah asked.

"There is a problem at my nightclub. There has been an argument and the police are called." He was obviously furious. "I am sorry Sarah but I have to go."

"Oh please. Just a few more minutes. They said they would be calling Pat soon." As she spoke, Sarah turned towards Luan and realised that the front of her top felt wet. Luan looked down at the same time, his face horrified.

"What is that?!" He pointed at the two wet patches forming on the material.

Sarah put her hands over her breasts in embarrassment, feeling the tingling release of milk.

"It's milk!" she said. "I need to feed my baby."

Luan stood up and backed away. "I have to go!" he said. "I have to go now!"

"But what about me? What about Pat? How will we get home?" Sarah stood up and moved towards him.

Luan pulled a wallet out of his pocket, his face still a picture of horror.

"Here!" He pushed a bundle of notes into Sarah's hands. "Get taxi when you finished here. I have to go, sort this out." He couldn't tear his eyes away from the milky patches.

Sarah held his hand for a moment as she grasped the notes. "Will you call me soon and we'll arrange something?" she said, unable to resist winding him up and safe in the knowledge that he never would now.

"Yes, yes, of course, of course. I go now." Luan's accent was getting thicker in his agitation. He turned and virtually ran out of the A & E department and out into the street.

Sarah sat down heavily in her seat. She had to phone Lizzie and Tony to let them know what had happened. It seemed likely that Luan would not bother them tonight if there were problems at his club, but she wanted them to know that she and Pat were alright. Then she needed to see Pat home and make sure she got into bed, then go on to her own home and her babies. She allowed herself a relieved smile.

"Looks like we can go now" she said, turning to look at Pat. Pat's head had fallen onto her chest and she was snoring gently.

Chapter 15

When Sami had left, Tony made sure the service door was locked then went back up the stairs.

"Sami's heading for the lock up in Selford now he's taken the key," Tony said.

"We need to get over there as quickly as possible." Titus was talking and James was zipping up his laptop case. "We've got all we can here."

"You need to get the other keys to Geoff now Tony," I said, "then get off home. Sarah will be in touch with you again before long, I'm sure."

Tony shook hands with Titus and James and I gave him a hug. "She'll be fine, Tony. She's handling things really well. We'll hear from her again soon." We started to leave and make our way down the corridor when all our phones buzzed with another message. It was Sarah.

"I'm in Sandra's car heading to take Pat home. I'll get a taxi back from there. Luan had to go to his club to handle some sort of problem which involved the police being called out. Trudy is heading for home in her car too."

Tony gave a relieved smile then saw us out of the service door and wished us luck.

"Take care. We'll all keep in touch," and he locked the door behind us, heading over to hand the keys to Geoff.

James took my car keys from me.

"I can drive quicker than you, Ma," he said. I didn't argue. I don't drive in the dark much these days and it was the early hours of the morning, way past my bedtime but probably not his. We had a short walk through deserted streets on the estate of office buildings to get back to the car park. I climbed into the rear seat and let Titus take the front passenger seat so that he could guide James back towards our little town and the lock up. It was about a forty minute drive, maybe more usually, but James certainly drove faster than I normally do. My little car almost flew. I was quite worried that we would be stopped for speeding but thankfully we weren't.

After about half an hour I had another message from Sarah. She was with Pat waiting for a taxi to pick her up from Pat's flat. She had messaged again because she wasn't sure if she should call in case Sami was nearby, but I called her back straight away.

"Thanks for calling, love. We're in my car on our way to see what Sami is up to. James is driving. He always was a frustrated racing driver." James took another corner at speed and I hung on to the handle above the door to avoid falling over.

"How are you and the Friday girls?"

"We're fine thanks, at least I will be as soon as I get home. Trudy just messaged to say she's back at her flat already.

"Pat is settled now. She was pretty tired so I've put her to bed. Sandra's a night owl so she's not so bad, but she headed home as soon as she dropped me and Pat. She offered to drive me home but it's a long journey and Luan had given me money for a taxi when he deserted us at the hospital so I decided to use it and let her get off home. I suppose I'm tired too, but I'm fired up on adrenaline at the moment, just so relieved we managed to keep Luan out of the way long enough for you to do everything you wanted to. Relieved I managed to keep him under control too. He left for his club in Leeds a while ago, some problem with a fight and the police being called."

"Tony will have left the office now," I said. "You should phone him. He will be so relieved to hear from you. He's been worried sick that Luan was going to be pawing you and not taking no for an answer!"

"Bless him. He's found it difficult. I must admit, it wasn't very pleasant sitting next to Luan and being all sweetness and light when I know what he's really like."

"You shouldn't have to see him again anyway. You did a good job." James was slowing the car down now.

"Look love, we're nearly there. We don't know what to expect at this lock up so better not phone us again. We'll get in touch with you as soon as we can. Send a message to everyone so no one calls us please. I might be too busy for a while. Try to get some sleep, all of you. Give everyone our love."

We were almost at the lock up now so we checked our phones were on silent. James had slowed the car right down and we crawled along the street with our lights out. We soon saw a small van parked at the side of the road. It was hard to see if the colour was blue under the streetlights, but it was parked near the lockup and there was nothing else around. James tucked the car into a side street and we all climbed out, hiding in the bushes. We crouched low as we crept towards the building. We passed the van, creeping along, and James tried the driver's door but it was locked. Titus tested the back doors but they were locked too.

"He must be in the building," whispered James. We could see a glow of light under the door. We had no way of knowing whether Sami had unloaded his cargo already or whether it was still in the van.

Suddenly there was a slight noise. We all froze, crouched down behind the van. There was the noise again. Was it a whimper or a muffled sob?

"It's coming from in the van," Titus mouthed, hardly breathing the words and pointing. "We need to get the keys. Sami must have taken them inside. They're probably in his pocket."

There was sound from inside the building. Maybe Sami was coming out again. We hurried into the bushes near the door entrance, the men to the left of the door and me to the right. There were a few moments of silence as we rallied our thoughts but not for long. The door opened letting a flood of light onto the short path and Sami took a step out.

"Benjie!" It was my voice, but not as I knew it. "Benjie! Where are you boy?!" I came out of the shrubs backwards, shining the torch from my phone into the leaves and backing towards Sami.

"Oh!" I jumped as I bumped into him and turned round, shining the torch into his face. "Sure you froightened the loif out of me! What a scare!" It must have been the worst Irish accent ever, but I hoped Sami's English was too poor to realise it was fake.

"What the . . .?!" Sami used a word I had never heard before, presumably an Albanian curse. "What you doing, you stupid old woman?"

He grabbed my wrist and lowered it so that the torch was pointing towards the ground.

"What am Oi doing? You eejit! I'm after foinding me dog, in't Oi. He's run off again and he's round here somewhere!" I shone the torch in his face again and caught a glimpse of James over Sami's left shoulder, looking at me with his head on one side and his eyes wide in surprise. He raised his right hand and I saw he was holding a half brick, lifting it high, presumably to smash Sami's head. A split second later, before the brick came down, Titus loomed over Sami's right shoulder. Shouldering James out of the way he gripped Sami's neck on both sides. Sami's legs crumpled and he fell forward onto his knees. Titus continued the pressure with his hands and Sami fell forward with his head on the grass at my feet.

My jaw had dropped open. I must stop that, it was not a good look.

"I didn't know people could really do that thing with the hands on the neck. I thought it was just something they did in films," I said, staring at Sami's body.

"An S.A.S. guy taught me how to do it, one drunken night in Kiev," said Titus. "Although, I honestly never thought I would actually do it. I wasn't sure it would work." We were all frozen for the moment, then Titus snapped back into action. "Shine that torch over here quickly, before he comes to. Let's check his pockets. We need those keys!"

James grabbed Sami's hands and held them together behind his back. "We need something to tie these together too," he said.

I put a hand reluctantly into Sami's right trouser pocket but pulled it out quickly. "Yeuk!" I yelped. "There's an animal in there!"

"Don't be an idiot, Ma! Or should I say eejit!? What animal could he possibly have in his pocket? You think he'd keep a rat in there?!"

"It's something furry, I tell you.   You look if you don't believe me!"

I shone the torch on the pocket and Titus moved round so he could get his hand to it.   Slowly he pulled out an object and held it up.   It was a set of very furry handcuffs.

"Well, well, well.   Not an animal at all, but a useful find, not to say telling about Mr Sami's interesting lifestyle.   Let's get these on him quickly, before he wakes up."

The two men clicked the handcuffs in place then James felt in Sami's left pocket and pulled out the bunch of keys and three small packets of white powder.   "Well, well, well, as you said Titus.   We learn yet more about our friend's habits.   None of it entirely surprising I suppose."   He put the powder in his pocket and passed the keys to me.   "Hold on to these a minute while we drag this guy into the bushes.   We need him where he can't see us if he comes round."

"I hope you're not saving that for personal use, are you?   It could be anything."   Titus was stating what I was thinking.

"Now who's being an eejit?   I'm not stupid.   But it might be useful for the boffins to analyse.   They can sometimes trace a particular supplier that way."

"Is he. . .is he alright?   I mean. . . he's not dead is he?"   I was not worried about the legality or otherwise of most of what we were doing.   We were trying to bring the bad guys to justice after all.   But murder might be more difficult to explain, or to live with.

"Nah, he's fine.   Yes, he's out cold at the moment, and he'll have a headache, but he'll come round soon.   We need to be quick."

We half pulled, half carried Sami deep into the bushes beside the building and out of sight from the road.   It took the three of us quite a while.   I'd always thought that they make it look too easy to move a heavy body in the films and I was right. It didn't help that we were fighting the low branches, but it was done eventually and we all stood panting, getting our breath, dusting off leaves and twigs and wondering what to do next.

James took the keys I was holding and looked at Titus. They nodded at each other then James said, "Wait here, Ma, while we check inside."

"No chance," I said. "I'm coming in too."

We all moved slowly towards the door and Titus pushed it further open. It didn't take long to establish that there was nothing of great interest there. Yes, it was full of cigarettes and crates of booze stacked all around and packs of foodstuffs, mostly cakes and biscuits I thought from the pictures on the packaging, but nothing out of the ordinary. Then we found a small room at the back.

Again we hesitated. The door was open slightly and we pushed it wider. I shone my phone torch into the room. There were scruffy sleeping bags on the floor, a bucket in the corner and an unopened pack of bottled water near the doorway. Titus walked carefully into the room, signalling me to shine the torch round to light the area behind the door. All clear. Then he beckoned me over to the bucket and pointed for me to light up the inside. Empty.

"So, he's prepared for someone to make an overnight stay," he whispered. "We need to look in the van."

He picked up the pack of bottled water then closed the door to the small room as we left and James found the key to lock it. We did the same to the external door of the lock up, Titus picking up a pack of something from the storeroom and handing it to me, then remembering to turn out the light as we left. We all had a good idea of what we thought might be in the van by now. I confess my knees were knocking at what we were going to see.

"You really do need to stand back now, Lizzie," said Titus. "Give me your phone." I passed it to him and he played the torchlight onto the keyhole of the back door as James looked for the key. James put his hand on the handle ready to open it but Titus held his hand up to stop him. He banged gently on the door.

"It's alright. The bad man has gone. We're here to help you."

He paused for a moment, but there was silence. He spoke again, this time in Albanian, presumably saying the same words. Again silence. He said something else, perhaps indicating that we would open the doors then nodded at James.

As James pulled on the handle Titus shone the torch into the back of the van. Huddled on the floor were four children. At first sight it was not clear if they were boys or girls. They all had tangled medium length hair and wore dirty tee shirts, jeans and trainers. At a guess three were twelve or thirteen years old, the fourth a little older, maybe sixteen. He, I was guessing this one was a boy, had his arm protectively round one of the girls and held a second by the hand. They all had skinny bodies and dark, sunken eyes, but he had a spark of defiance in his, a readiness to fight, or protect his colleagues. The smell of unwashed bodies was overwhelming and I put my hand over my mouth and nose.

Titus spoke again in Albanian. I don't know what he said but the boy listened and eventually nodded. Titus turned to James. "They need water," he said. James put the bottles into the van. "And they're hungry." He looked at the pack I was holding. It looked like some sort of biscuit or cake but the writing was foreign to me so I wasn't sure exactly what. I stepped forward and put that on the floor of the van too. The boy's eyes were watching us all. Slowly, keeping a wary eye on us, he leaned forward and pulled the water bottles towards him, tore and stretched the plastic wrapping and handed the girls a bottle each, then took one himself. They drank thirstily, but all kept an eye on us.

James tore open the wrapping on the pack of cakes and pulled the smaller packages out holding them out to each of the children. Hesitantly they opened these and began to eat.

"They need proper food and a good wash," I said. "Are they hurt? Do they need to go to hospital?"

Titus spoke to them again and the boy shook his head. There was more conversation which James and I couldn't understand so we took a step backwards and spoke to each other.

"What happens now?" I said. "These poor kids need help, more than we can give them."

"We'll have to hand them over to the authorities I suppose." He looked round and in the direction of the bushes where we had left Sami. "We ought to get them away from here though. If Sami wakes up he will start making a noise and someone will eventually come along and find him."

The boy had moved forward to crouch on the edge of the van now, helping himself to more water and food as he talked to Titus. James moved towards the van.

"Let's get them away from here. We need to call the authorities and hand them over but we should make sure none of Luan's bully boys come looking for them while we're still here."

Titus was still talking to the boy and seemed to be putting something in his hand. He nodded at him then turned his back and talked to James and me, taking a step away from the van. Suddenly, the boy sprang from the back of the van and sprinted down the road.

The older looking girl got on her knees and fell forward onto her hands, leaning out of the van. She was shouting something after him, panic in her voice and face. Titus and I moved towards her, frightened she too would bolt, or fall from the van. James made as if to run after the boy, but Titus grabbed his arm.

"Let him go, James," he said. "He would leg it eventually anyway. He's got contacts in Bradford. He'll just disappear."

The boy had stopped in the shadows further up the road and turned round. He shouted a reply to the girl and she called to him again. They shouted to each other a few times, their voices emotional. She was in tears and, to be honest, so was I.

"What's going on?" I asked. "What are they saying?"

"She doesn't want him to leave her. She's scared. She's his sister. He's told her we're not the bad guys. That she'll be alright if she stays with us."

We all looked as he stood, hesitating. Then he shouted again, waved, turned and vanished into the darkness.

"What did he say?" It was James asking this time.

"He said he will find her. Wherever they take her, he will find her."

It took us all a few moments to gather our thoughts. I put my hand on the girl's shoulder and offered her a tissue from my pocket to wipe her eyes.

"Should we put them in my car and take them to my house?" I couldn't get the smell out of my nostrils and wanted to get them in a bath or shower quickly.

"There are only three of them and they're skinny little things. We could squeeze them in."

"Not a good idea," said Titus. "Unless you want your car to smell like a doss house for the next month. And they could well have livestock that you don't want embedded in your cushions."

"Oh, you mean nits? Well, nits and lice. Yes. I suppose so."

"Maybe fleas too. Best if I keep them in the van and we take them straight upstairs to your bathroom when we get there." Titus paused. "That's assuming you're ok with them being taken back to your house till the authorities come and pick them up?"

"Oh, Titus, of course. Look at them. They're frightened witless. Can you explain what we're going to do?"

Titus turned back to the girls and spoke slowly to them, pointing to me, and to where we had hidden Sami. The girls listened, wide eyed, then slid back into the van as he closed and locked the van doors.

"Do you really need to lock them in now?" I was sure the sound of the key turning would be frightening for them. Locked in again.

"I don't know how safe the doors are for a start. They could fly open as we're travelling. Or they could just make a run for it if I'm stopped at traffic lights, or even if the van's moving. They've no real reason to trust us. They don't know who to trust. They might just decide to take their chances."

James and I walked back up the road to my car as Titus climbed in the driver's seat of the van. I stopped, then ran back to the van.

"We'll pass the superstore on the way back to my house. It's open twenty four hours." Titus had wound down the window and I was leaning in to talk to him. "I want to call there. I can get medicated shampoo and some clean clothes for them."

Titus nodded. "Get bread and soup too, unless you already have it." I turned to go. "Lizzie!" I turned back. "I'm sorry to bring this to your door."

I smiled. "Don't be silly. You didn't bring this, it was already here. We're just doing something about it."

Half an hour later I was back at the car with carrier bags full of shampoo, underclothes, jogging trousers and sweatshirts. I'd even bought trainers, taking a guess at all the sizes. I threw the bags onto the back seat and James pulled away heading for home, the blue van following us.

Chapter 16

We pulled up in the two vehicles outside my house and Titus opened the back doors of the van while I opened my kitchen door. We led the girls straight up to my bathroom and James brought up the bags of clothes. I made a big thing of taking the bags from him and shoo-ing him out of the bathroom, sending him back down the stairs and closing the door behind him, so the girls could see that there would not be a man in the room. They watched, wide eyed.

The girls huddled together, looking around at my bathroom. I smiled and pointed to the shower. I moved over and started the water running, handing one of them a plastic bottle of shower gel, after taking the top off first and exaggeratedly miming smelling the perfume. Smiling all the time like a demented mime artist I turned back to the bags and shook out the clothes. I lifted an empty bag and said, "Put your old clothes in the bags." I pointed and shook the bag. "Put your old clothes in the bag, then go in the shower." I pointed to the shower. "It will feel so good to be clean. Please."

The girls looked at each other.

I grabbed some of the clean clothes and held them up.

"You can put these on when you've had a shower." I pointed again to the shower and smiled, nodding. Slowly, the tallest of the girls moved away from the others. She bent down and unfastened her shoes, then stripped off her jeans. I held out the bag and she dropped them in. Slowly, all three girls stripped off and climbed into the shower. I turned my back and began to gather the dirty clothes from the floor.

Some time later we were all in my kitchen. The smell of chicken soup had been reaching our nostrils for the last few minutes and the girls sat down at the table, where Titus had laid out bread, chunks of cheese, small slices of ham and chorizo, plates, soup bowls and spoons. I ladled soup into the bowls as James came through the kitchen door, putting his jacket on the back of one of the dining chairs.

"I left the van behind that tall hedge in the field near the canal," he said. "Someone will report it as an abandoned vehicle in the morning when they're walking their dog, but I've let London know and our guys will probably retrieve it before the local police get round to it anyway."

"It's morning now," said Titus. We looked out of the window and realised that dawn was breaking.

The girls were eating hungrily and I topped up all the bowls as they emptied them. Titus had made coffee for us and put three glasses and a jug of water on the table for the girls. He poured our coffees then turned and leaned against the sink. "We need to stay awake, make sure that these three don't go AWOL."

I waited but he didn't speak. I looked from James to Titus.

"What happens now?"

Titus helped himself to a coffee and poured milk into it. "I phoned my contacts. They're sending social services to collect them. Might be a while before they get here so best to let them sleep when they finish eating." I nodded. "But James is right, we need to keep an eye on them till someone gets here."

I picked up my coffee and added milk then stood up to pull a plastic box down from the cupboard. I pulled a knife from a drawer. Three shocked gasps made me realise how bad that looked. Sitting down at the table I opened the box and smiled at the girls. "Who likes homemade cake?"

We all sat and chatted, smiling and gesturing, trying to make them feel as comfortable as we could. It reminded me of times we had shared with school exchange students over the years. We'd had a variety of French and German schoolboys and girls sitting round this table. Most of them could speak some English of course and we could speak some French and German, though not fluently. Now I was smiling broadly, nodding and gesturing in an exaggerated way in a vain attempt at making tonight feel normal. I suddenly realised how ridiculous this was. As I put the last piece of cake on my plate I began to giggle. A gentle, low noise at first, then louder. Titus gave me a shocked look, then smiled, then he began to laugh too. The girls looked from one to the other, then gradually they relaxed and they too smiled and eventually all six of us were laughing, eating and drinking in this most absurd of situations.

Later, when I had put the girls to bed, we three sat talking round the table, drinking more coffee and trying to stay awake.

"I'm assuming you talked to Tony and Sarah and they're safe and aware of what's happened?"

Titus nodded. "Yeah, they're fine. I called Sarah a while back to fill her in and she was just pulling up to her drive in a taxi and she could see Tony's van parked outside the house. They'll be trying to catch some sleep now, I should think. Their children will be awake soon."

"I sent texts to all the Friday girls to let them know everybody is alright. I thought it was a bit much to expect them to be sitting up and waiting for a call and it didn't seem fair to wake them. They will pick up their messages soon, when they wake up. It is morning after all."

"Those girls all got into the shower together you know, and laughed and talked while they were washing their hair like any other children do. They looked angelic, tucked up under the duvet, all in one big bed, all clean and tidy. It reminded me of Christmas holidays years ago, when we used to meet up with your cousins James and you boys had to share one bed and the girls snuggled up in another."

"I hate to spoil the image," said Titus, "and I'm not suggesting they should have been treated the way they have by Luan and his gangs, but these girls will be a lot more streetwise than your children ever were. Don't get all dreamy eyed about looking after them here. We're doing the right thing handing them over."

"So how come you turned a blind eye when the boy went then?" This was James, looking very heavy eyed and leaning back in his chair.

Titus looked sheepish. "Don't know what you mean," he said. "He took me completely by surprise when he scarpered." He was not making eye contact with either of us and stood up to help himself to more coffee.

"And I wonder how he got hold of that cash," I said, staring hard at him.

"Cash?" James raised one eyebrow.

"Mmm. I'm sure he had something in his hand as he ran off and I mean as well as the bottle of water he was holding. It looked very much like a couple of twenty pound notes." We were both silent for a minute, thinking our own thoughts. Slowly, Titus turned round, sat down again, and eventually spoke.

"He told me he has contacts in Bradford." Silence again.

"The girls will be fine. The system will kick in around them, but it's hard to sort out exactly what's happened. They could have been picked up from the streets, run away from abusive homes, even sold by their families."

I gasped. "Sold?!"

"It's a much bigger and more complicated problem than we can sort out, Lizzie. It was impossible to turn our backs to what was happening tonight, we had to stop Sami taking this 'load of merchandise' on anywhere. And we've done a good thing. But we can't be there for every case. It's happening all the time."

Titus took another sip of coffee.

"What we've found in Luan's office is going to be far more valuable to the people who can trace the forward and backward trail than saving individual kids, as callous as that sounds. And James will follow the money trail too. You've been part of something tonight that will make a difference, Lizzie."

I sipped my coffee again. Thinking about the girls upstairs, it didn't feel like we'd made much of a difference, but it was good to know that we might have had some effect on the bigger picture.

We all sat deep in our own thoughts, till a knock on the door signalled the arrival of Social Services.

****

Sarah had arrived safely back at home while all this was going on. She had been dropped off by the taxi and rushed up the drive, passing Tony's van. Tony appeared in the hallway as she turned to lock it, still wearing his paint splattered overalls.

"Thank goodness you're back," he said. "I've been worried sick."

Without pausing to look at him, she grabbed his hand and pulled him up the stairs. "I'm fine," she said. "Come upstairs though. I'm so glad to be here. I can't wait."

In their bedroom she immediately started to strip off the halter necked top, but struggled with the long straps that tied at the back of her neck. She had made sure they were securely knotted before she went out, so there was no danger of them coming unfastened either by accident or with Luan's help. Now they were proving more secure than she wanted.

"For goodness sake, get me out of this!" she hissed, not wanting to wake the rest of the household. She had her back to Tony and held her hair out of the way so Tony could help her.

Tony, not quite sure what was going on, stepped forward and untied the knots. Turning round as she let the top fall to the floor she threw her arms round Tony's neck, the relief of being back home with her loving husband overwhelming her. He pulled her close, glad to have her safe in his arms and still not quite believing what was happening. Surely, after the stress of the evening, and the late night, this was the time to expect a justifiable 'I'm too tired' type of comment. Sarah pulled her head back from his chest and looked up at him.

"I love you," she said.

He let one hand slide up to cup her breast, and bent his head to kiss her on the lips.

"Tony!" She pulled away and spoke loudly in her surprise. "What on earth are you doing? We haven't got time for that now!" She took a couple of steps back from him and wriggled out of the silky trousers. "Get Samuel up for me while I get out of this torturous g-string. It's been cutting me in two all night! And my boobs are almost bursting. I need to feed Sam before they explode!"

Tony sheepishly slipped into Samuel's bedroom, tiptoeing so he didn't wake up Jacob, who was sleeping on a mattress on the floor, while Sarah's mum was using his bedroom. He grinned to himself, as he realised how he had misread the signals.

A few minutes later, he was watching his wife, seated on the bedroom chair, feeding Samuel and sipping the glass of water he had brought her from the bathroom. She was comfortably relaxed now in her pyjamas and looking lovingly at Samuel.

Tony crouched on his haunches and stroked Samuel's hair, then put his hand behind Sarah's head, reached up and kissed her. "I love you too," he said, "so much."

Sarah smiled at him, then said the words she had said for the first time as they were alone at last in their bedroom on their wedding night. "You're my favourite husband."

Tony grinned. "Well, that's a relief."

A short while later, after Samuel was fed, changed and back in his cot, Tony then Sarah had showered, they lay side by side in bed exchanging information about the events of the evening and night, until gradually, they both fell silent and closed their eyes.

It seemed only minutes later that Jacob came bouncing into their bedroom.

Tony groaned as Jacob's knee found the tenderest part of his anatomy, a talent the three year old seemed to have perfected.

"Jacob, be careful," he mumbled, still reluctant to wake fully, despite the pain. "Go back to bed for a bit longer, it's early."

"Daddy! Wake up!" Jacob was wriggling into bed between Tony and Sarah with determination. Sarah moaned and pulled the duvet over her head, but, as the memory of last night surfaced in her brain, she poked her head out again, looked at her watch, then threw the cover back.

"Come on Jacob," she said. "Let's leave Daddy to have a bit more sleep. Remember he's been working for the last few nights so he needs to sleep during the day." She reached for her dressing gown as Tony opened one eye.

"Are you sure you're okay?" he asked. "You were up late last night as well."

"I'm fine," she said. "I slept in the taxi on the way back for half an hour and I'm used to having minimum sleep since I became a mother. Mum's here don't forget, so I need to get up so she can leave. She'll have to be off to work soon, and Samuel will be ready for a feed again before too long anyway." She smiled, remembering the events of the previous night as she picked up her clothes, discarded in such a hurry.

Now, after minimal sleep and saying goodbye with grateful thanks to her mum, she was back to her normal routine: getting breakfast for Jacob, feeding Samuel and sorting out the washing, including the borrowed outfit from last night. The evening spent with Luan seemed like a long time in the past. But she and Tony had exchanged enough information before they went to sleep to know that what they had been part of could have big implications. Each had only part of the story, but together they had a good idea of how the night had progressed. Sarah even had a text she had picked up this morning from Lizzie giving brief details about what, or rather who, had been in Sami's van. She would show it to Tony when he woke up. She assumed Lizzie, James and Titus would also be sleeping now. They'd had a longer night than anyone. She sent Lizzie a quick text to say she and Tony were fine and they could talk later when they were all awake.

Later still, after she'd had lunch and fed Samuel again she put him down for his afternoon nap. A friend had rung to see if Jacob would like to come and play with her little boy for the afternoon. He was at his friend's now and she was due to pick him up again in two hours. She took Tony a mug of tea and was pleased to see he was stirring as she went into the bedroom. She sat on the side of the bed to talk to him.

"Oh thanks, love. I'm ready for a cuppa. You must be shattered. Do you want me to get up and you can have a couple of hours in bed while I look after the kids?"

"No need. Samuel's gone down in his cot for his afternoon nap just now and Jacob is at Ryan's house till later this afternoon."

Tony was sitting up, relishing his tea. She looked at him with a frown.

"What was that all about last night?" She was half smiling, half frowning at him.

"Oh I don't know." He was sheepish. "Put it down to lack of sleep and a very strange night. Not to mention being worried sick about you being with that creep."

"Oh creep is it now? Well at least you've realised that." She smiled. "So nothing to do with being jealous then?"

"'Course I was jealous. You don't know how hot you look in that outfit! Then, when you grabbed me and pulled me upstairs, I suppose I just got my wires crossed. I thought all my birthdays had come at once!"

Sarah stood up. Not fully awake yet, he gradually became aware that she was pulling her tee shirt over her head. How did women do that Tony wondered, crossing their arms and wriggling the shirt over their heads? Men just grabbed theirs at the back of their neck and yanked it up and over.

He must still be half asleep. Sarah was reaching behind her back to unclip her bra now. That was another thing women could do, fasten and unfasten things behind their backs. He was suddenly fully awake and sait up straighter in bed, putting his mug of tea on the bedside table. After the fiasco of last night he was still uncertain he was reading the signals right, but Sarah was smiling at him now and stepping out of her jogging trousers.

"Well come on lover boy," she said. "Move over. It must be your birthday!"

Chapter 17

Social Services took the girls away that night, or rather morning. I was so sorry to see them go. They were clean and rested but still looked like frightened rabbits. No matter how streetwise they might be, this must have been a traumatic period in their lives. I really hoped they would have a good future. Tony and his family were a success story. They were examples of how asylum seekers could make a new life, but their circumstances were very different to these poor girls. I would probably never know how their lives progressed.

I did get a bit of a ticking off for having let them have showers and new clothes. They were supposed to be picked up as they were. Ideally, we should have kept them in the van till they were collected. As if we were going to do that. I told the social workers that I wasn't having the girls in my bed till they were showered and in clean clothes. I had kept their clothes, one bag for each girl's things, so they could see them and do whatever they needed to with them. Forensic examination to track anyone who had been involved in trafficking them if you can believe what you see on the films. Or maybe I am being too hopeful. Perhaps I should stop watching so much TV.

After the girls had gone, James, Titus and I slept for hours.

Even when we woke up we were in a daze. It took all three of us ages to come round and speak in coherent sentences. We were waiting to see what happened next.

I had a quick chat with the Friday girls, and talked to Sarah and Tony, so we were all up to speed. A lot depended on what was gleaned from the information we had found. James was trawling through the financial stuff and had passed a lot of the other details on to other specialists he worked with. Titus said his contacts were looking for leads about who else was involved. They wouldn't do anything until they felt they knew as much as they could. They didn't want anyone getting early warning of how much they knew.

As usual, I was on refreshment duty.

I put a coffee on the table next to James' laptop and peered at the figures on his screen.

"Is it going to be helpful?" I asked hopefully.

"You bet, Ma. Some of this stuff is dynamite," he said, not taking his eyes off the screen, his fingers flying over the keys. "There's a money trail here leading to lots of cash."

"Is Luan really rich then?" I asked. "I thought he was just a sleazy small town crook"

"He is, but he's moving into the big time, and he's been stashing cash away then investing it with the bigger boys. I've found lots of incriminating emails, contact details and best of all, money he was trying to launder but wasn't very good at it. I can follow the trail really easily, then move on to trawling through the bigger fish he's put us on to. There'll be even bigger money there. My bosses are going to be really pleased with me."

I put another coffee at the other end of the table next to Titus, then sat next to him with mine. He too was on his laptop.

"I don't suppose there's any news of the girls?" I was not really hopeful but it was worth asking.

"No, sorry Lizzie," he said. "I think you're going to have to accept that you won't hear. Let it go."

He paused and looked at my disappointed face as he picked up his mug.

"Keep remembering you made a difference though. They're safe. Think where they would be if you hadn't helped them."

"That's exactly what I'm trying not to think about!" I said.

"Well, as James said, we got some terrific leads. There are going to be raids all over the U.K. and some pretty worried gangland bosses wondering how the authorities found out so much."

I hoped that would happen soon. We would all feel better if Luan, Sami and their associates were in custody and couldn't follow up any leads to us.

In the end we waited several days before we all gathered together again. By that time it almost seemed like a dream, something we had imagined, but eventually we had a meeting at my house. Once we were all seated and everyone had a glass of something in their hands, James set the ball rolling.

"Good evening everybody. It's really great to have everyone here. I want to thank you on behalf of my bosses. They don't know exactly what you did, best not to be too specific, but they know that you all helped in a successful operation. Well done everyone." James raised his glass in a toast and we all followed suit.

We were sitting in my lounge, me, James, Titus, Tony, Sarah, Sandra, Pat and Trudy.

"I really enjoyed myself," said Trudy. "That security guard was a pushover."

"Has he tried to phone you?" asked Pat. "You gave him your number didn't you?"

"No chance," said Trudy. "I made that mistake when I was about sixteen. I never give my real number to anyone when I first meet them. If I'm interested, I get them to give me their number. Then I can follow up if I still think they're worth it in the cold light of day. If not, I can delete it."

"I just have to make sure I stay away from his favourite haunts. Shouldn't be difficult. He told me all about where he usually hangs out and they're not my sort of places anyway."

Once more, we were impressed with Trudy's handling of the situation.

"I'm raising my glass to you again Trudy," said Titus. "If they'd known about you forty years ago, my contacts would have been trying to recruit you."

Trudy bowed her head, acknowledging the compliment.

"How do you know they didn't?" she said. "Oxbridge isn't the only place they recruit from, you know. I used to work on cruise ships. You'd be surprised what goes on there and what you can find out. People will tell their hairdresser their secrets without thinking twice." She gave a sly smile and sipped her drink.

There was a long pause. None of us were quite sure whether to believe her or not, but we all felt it could be true. She looked round at us all then grinned.

"Your faces!" she said and laughed.

She was joking. Was she joking? Surely she was joking. We would probably never know.

"Well I'm glad they didn't try to recruit me," said Pat. "I had quite enough excitement in just that one night to last me a lifetime. I couldn't tell you what the show was about. I was so nervous, I couldn't watch it at all. And I wish I knew who pushed me down the stairs. I was just about to do the pretend stumble that I'd practised when someone gave me a huge shove! It's a wonder I didn't break my neck!"

We all tried not to look at Sandra, who was busy studying the bottom of her glass.

"Well the big news I have is that, as we speak, Luan has been arrested."

We all turned our faces to Titus now.

"I had word earlier today that tonight's the night for multiple raids. You might not hear much about it, they'll keep things as quiet as they can till they have to bring it all into the light, but I can assure you that there's lots happening."

"Does that mean I can relax now?" said Tony. "I've been expecting Luan to contact me any time, asking what I have done. Are Sarah and I really safe now? He doesn't know we had anything to do with it?"

"He doesn't know anyone here was involved," said James, and Titus nodded too.

"We want him to think it was someone from his world that blew it all up for him. People can never trust each other in the lifestyle he leads. He'll expect it to be one of them and spend the rest of his life trying to work it out."

"Well, I can't pretend I'm not relieved," said Sarah. "We were both worried that he might guess that Tony had informed on him." She looked up at Tony who was sitting on the arm of her chair.

"No chance," said Titus. "He gave his keys to so many people, for a start, including Geoff and Sami. Sami had lost his on the night we were in action, or so he said. Luan will remember that and probably suspect him most of all, especially since he lost the van with the girl's in it. The boy too as far as he knows. Tony was the one he would least suspect. He sees him as a squeaky clean guy, which is what he is." Sarah smiled at Tony. "In fact, I think he quite admires Tony's honesty."

"Didn't stop his lusting after Sarah though, did it? No loyalty there!" said Tony, and we all nodded.

"That reminds me," said Sarah, picking up a carrier bag from the side of her chair. "Here is your trouser suit, Trudy. Thanks for lending it to me for the night."

"Oh, don't worry about that," said Trudy. "I haven't worn it for years. It's a bit too young for me these days. I have to wear something that covers my bingo wings."

"You don't have bingo wings!" Sandra, Pat and I spoke in chorus.

"Well, not bad ones," Trudy conceded, "but I won't wear it again anyway. You keep it Sarah."

"Oh I don't think it's my sty . . . " Sarah began, holding out the bag.

"That's really kind of you," said Tony, snatching the bag and putting it back on the floor near his feet. "Thank you very much."

I topped up all the drinks while everyone chatted. When I sat down again, Tony cleared his throat and we all looked at him.

"Actually, I wanted to ask for advice about something. You'll remember that Luan left some money in his desk drawer for me in a brown envelope. Payment for the decorating work I did in the offices for him. I know it's a fair price for what I did but. . . ." He took the envelope out of his pocket. "I don't like taking it. Sarah and I talked about it and it feels like dirty money. What should we do with it?"

Titus shook his head.

"You should take it. You earned it honestly. You worked all those nights and did a good job from what I saw. You deserve it."

"But if Luan earned it by selling drugs or worse, I don't want it. I know I've taken money for work I've done for him in the past, but it feels different now. I know how he earned some of his money now."

"I know it's payment for decorating work, but it just feels wrong. And I know it's stupid but I still feel like I was disloyal to him. Don't get me wrong, he deserves everything that they can throw at him. But I still feel I was going behind his back and ratting on him."

James took the envelope from Tony, who was holding it out.

"Look Tony. We don't know exactly where this money came from. Luan has clean businesses as well as grubby ones. Chances are this is clean money because you were doing an above board job in his new premises. Even if you tried to hand it over, who would you give it to? You were not officially involved in this caper, neither you nor Sarah. You worked long hours and paid for the materials up front yourself."

"As for being loyal, he wasn't loyal to you, trying to seduce Sarah. You know he didn't want to take her out to give her a treat. He would have had her in his bed quite happily, not a thought about being disloyal to you."

Sarah blushed and held Tony's hand.

"No he wouldn't have, because I never would."

"We know that Sarah. No one here has any doubt about that, but that's what he wanted."

Titus took the envelope from James now.

"Take it, Sarah. It's better in your pocket, paying your bills, than just being added to a huge chunk of money that's going to get confiscated from his accounts." He held out the envelope to Sarah, who looked at Tony. He nodded and Sarah took it and put it into her bag.

"I can't say it won't be useful. Thanks."

James stood up and walked to the back of the room. He picked up his laptop case and carried it over to me as I sat in my chair.

"Hold this for a few minutes for me please, Ma while I sort a few things out."

He took several envelopes from the case then looked round the room. Everyone waited, wondering what was coming next.

"Well folks, I have to love you and leave you shortly. I'm booked on the train down to London in an hour." James looked down at me. "I'm going to miss you Ma, but I promise I will be back soon." He smiled at me and reached down to squeeze my hand. This wasn't a surprise. James had told me earlier that he had to leave and had booked his train ticket. I had helped him to pack his bag and ordered a taxi to take him to the station. I still felt my eyes fill with tears at the thought of having to say goodbye to my youngest son but I would worry about him much less now that I knew he was well established in his work. Work that I was proud he was involved in, even if I could never tell anyone exactly what he was doing, even some of the people in the room with me.

James turned back to them all now.

"In the meantime, I'm glad to know that you have good friends here and a special person in your life who will take care of you." He turned to Titus this time and they nodded solemnly at each other.

"Now," he looked round at everyone again, "I know that you understand that we can never talk to anyone else about what we all did. Never," he repeated, "Not to anyone; not to family, or friends or strangers you meet on holiday and think you will never see again." He looked round at each of us in turn, giving us all hard stares.

"But that doesn't mean you shouldn't get some acknowledgement or thanks for what you did. There is one of these envelopes for everyone. Each one contains a little something that we hope will show our gratitude."

He moved round the room handing out the envelopes, one each to Trudy, Sandra and Pat first.

"Most of these are vouchers, so you can choose dates to suit yourselves. And you might want to arrange to use them at the same time as each other."

He handed an envelope to Titus next, then one to me and gave us both a cheeky wink as he moved round the room.

The last two envelopes were for Sarah and Tony.

"Who exactly are these from?" asked Sandra.

James smiled at her.

"Let's just say, from Luan and his friends, via me and my friends. I can't say more than that."

"Oh fantastic!" Trudy was the first to open her envelope. "A weekend at the Spa Hotel in Harrogate! With four free treatments too." She started to look at the brochure detailing the treatments. "Oh great! It includes botox!"

"I've got that too," said Sandra. "It's a champagne weekend with afternoon tea on arrival."

"Oh good, I've got the same!" Pat was flushed with excitement. "I've always wished I could afford a day at a spa. A whole weekend and champagne too!" She was studying the leaflet. "I'm not sure about botox but the special pedicure sounds lovely."

"The pool looks fantastic. I'll be in there every day. And look at that gym!" This was Sandra again.

Trudy pulled a face. "Meet you in the jacuzzi, that looks more my style."

By this time I had opened my envelope. "I've got the same package," I said. "We can have a girly weekend. I love it!" and I jumped up to give James a hug. "How on earth did you get your bosses to authorise this?"

James looked a bit sheepish. "I'll explain all about that later. Don't worry about it now."

He was looking at Titus, who was deliberately avoiding his eye. His mouth was turning up slightly at the corners though, so I let it go.

"What's in your envelope Titus?" I sat down next to him again and tried to look at the papers in his hand.

"Are you coming to the Spa with us too?" Trudy was grinning cheekily. "We'll make room for you in the jacuzzi."

"'Fraid I'll have to disappoint you there." Titus waved the brochure he had pulled from his envelope. "I've got a weekend break in Paris, travelling on the Eurostar. Oh dear," he paused and looked at the leaflet carefully. "It's for two people. I'll have to find someone to come with me."

I blushed as the three women on the sofa smirked and nudged each other.

"I did think about a weekend in London for you Titus, with 2 tickets for the Wimbledon final, but I think you've already got that covered anyway." James was grinning at me as he spoke and Titus smiled across at me. I raised my eyebrows questioningly and he grinned back..

"What about you, Sarah?" I was eager to take the focus of attention away from me and Titus.

"A weekend for two in London, including train travel and staying at a posh looking hotel. She was flushed with excitement but still looking through the papers. "Oh and it includes a show!" She was obviously thrilled but Tony's face showed he was less so.

"The weekend deal sounds great but do we have to do a show?" he said, less than enthusiastically.

Sarah nudged him. "I know what we'll go to see. 'Chicago.'"

"What?" he said, looking puzzled. "That was the show you went to with Luan."

"Yes, but I couldn't enjoy it with him. I was on edge all the time. I'd love to see it when I can relax and be comfortable. And actually, I think you'd enjoy it too. Those girls are gorgeous, so glamorous. They have figures to die for and their legs go on forever!" She was smiling at him.

"Oh dear, am I so predictable?" He smiled back.

"We'll have to wait till Samuel is a bit older and I've finished breast feeding, so Mum can look after the children for the weekend." Sarah was planning ahead. "But it will be fabulous to have some special time together, just us."

"Yeah, the whole deal will be great. I can't remember when we last had time out together. And we could never afford something like this. Thanks James."

A thought occurred to him. "And you could wear the outfit Trudy's just given you." He and Trudy exchanged knowing looks.

There was a general murmur of approval and thanks for all the gifts.

"Just you left then Tony. What have you got?" This was Sandra asking.

Tony shuffled the papers as he looked through them, Sarah looking at them as he held them down for her to see too. There didn't seem to be any glossy brochures among them.

"I'm not quite sure I understand." He sounded puzzled and was pointing out something on one of the sheets to Sarah. She took it from him with a puzzled frown.

"Maybe I should explain." James was looking at his watch. "My taxi will be here any time so keep an ear open please folks, but if you two come through to the kitchen I'll talk you through it."

Chapter 18

I went to stand by the window to watch for the car arriving, but there was a general buzz of conversation as we looked at our brochures and chatted about options.

Five minutes later the taxi pulled up at the bottom of the drive and tooted his car horn.

"James, it's here," I called as I went to open the front door and wave, to let the driver know we had seen him.

James came into the hall from the kitchen and picked up his bag as I handed him his laptop case.

"What was all that about in the kitchen?" I asked. "Is everything alright?"

"Titus will explain later, when you're on your own." James was putting the laptop strap across his body. "He knows all about it. Don't worry, it's all fine."

"I'm going to miss you, Ma, but I promise I'll be back soon." He was giving me a huge hug. "Or maybe you'll come and see me on one of your jaunts to London, you and Titus."

"I'll miss you too, but I won't worry now, at least not for the same reasons. I know you're not my black sheep anymore. You're my man in a white hat. Well done, love. I'm proud of you."

"I'm proud of you too Ma. But then, I always have been," and he was off, down the path and into the taxi.

We had another hour or so talking through everything and eating the supper I had made earlier, then the Friday girls left in their taxi. Sarah and Tony had been a little subdued since their talk with James but everyone had been tactful enough to avoid asking any questions. When we were on our own, though, Sarah looked at Tony and nudged him. He cleared his throat and said, "Titus, James said you know about this." He had taken the envelope out again and held it out for Titus to take. Titus looked at it before answering.

"I had a good idea but not the exact amount." He handed it back to Tony.

"What do you think? Should we take it?"

Titus's face was serious and thoughtful. "I think so Tony. I know it seems a lot to you, but it's a drop in the ocean to the people we're pulling in tonight."

I began to feel I was eavesdropping, but if this involved James I really wanted to stay.

"Excuse me," I said. "Is this something I should know about or would you prefer me to leave the room? I can go and start washing up."

"No, please stay," said Sarah. "You have a wise head. We value your opinion."

"Can you show Lizzie the statements?" said Titus and Tony passed the envelope to me.

I took a few minutes to look through everything then said, "Ok, so what I can see is paperwork for a bank account in joint names, for Sarah and Tony. There's some detail of it being set up several years ago and a balance of over £50,000. Am I to gather that you didn't know you had this account?"

"We didn't have this account," said Sarah, "at least, not until about an hour ago."

Titus didn't agree. "But everything here says you did. This paperwork is never going to be questioned, Sarah. James has assured me of that and I have no reason to doubt him. This money has come from the millions which will be pulled in after all this is cleared up. James assures me that this little 'bonus' you have been given will never be traced from them to you. Everything online confirms what you have in your hands. James has found lots of cash, filtered off through accounts in Jersey, the Cayman Islands and so on, moved and moved again and never traced. He's just moved a very small proportion of it into an account in your name before the rest gets seized by the authorities."

"James is particularly clever at his job. He knows what will be found and what won't. He hasn't done anything to put you in any danger. He believes you deserve this for the risks you took, you and Tony. And if my opinion counts for anything, I think so too. Let's put it this way, if your father were here Tony, I believe he'd tell you to take it."

Tony suddenly looked at Titus with an intensity that surprised me.

"You knew my father didn't you? It was you wasn't it? You got him out of that prison camp?"

"Titus?" No-one had spoken for a long time. "Titus, is that true?" I asked.

Tony smiled. "Of course it's true. He just doesn't want to say so, but I've been suspecting it for a while. The more I've got to know about him, the more likely it seemed. Then, recently, I found some old diaries of my father's, from when he was first in England. He wrote some things down but didn't speak of them. I hadn't looked at them for years but I found them out when I was looking for the photographs I brought for you to show to Emma. I read through them again yesterday."

"A lot of what he says in them doesn't make sense. I think his mind was confused, he was still ill, from time to time. But he mentions someone called Titus. He says, 'Titus did it. I don't know how, but he got us out.'"

"Titus...Titus...How many people, who happen to be working in that area as reporters, happen to be called Titus?"

"Your father was a good man," said Titus. "As I said, he would have wanted you to take this money."

It took me a while to take all this in. I had felt like that a lot recently. But then I had just one question.

"Titus, are you absolutely sure this is quite safe? It's not going to cause Tony and Sarah any problems in the future, or James either?"

Titus shook his head. "I've made enquiries. James is the best man in the country at tracing laundered money, the old way and the new way, with bitcoin and such. I can't say a hundred percent, of course. Nothing in life is a hundred percent. But if James has moved it into this account and says its source is untraceable, I'd stake my life on it being ok, and yours." He looked across at me and smiled. "And I wouldn't do that lightly."

I folded the papers and put them back into the envelope then handed them to Sarah. "Keep it," I said. "Actually, thinking about it, I don't know how you could hand it back anyway. It would be even more complicated than giving back the cash, and probably cause us all more problems too."

"No, keep it. There's enough there for a deposit on a nice little house in this area. Think about Jacob and Samuel. It would mean you could get your own place and a secure future for them. In fact," I was thinking again, "I don't actually know what will happen to all Luan's properties. It could be that you might have to leave your house soon, if his houses have to be sold. You might have to find somewhere else anyway. What do you think, Titus?"

"Most likely his property empire will be sold off at a bargain price. You could end up being able to buy the house you're renting now. I can find out a bit more for you if you like. Might take a while but keep the money in that account till then, it's earning the best interest around."

"But how can we explain it?" asked Sarah. "Not long ago we had to go to the food bank. Family and close friends know we were hard up. We were asking around for work because Tony didn't have a job. How can we justify doing all that if we had all this money sitting in a bank account?"

"Well, of course, you didn't actually have it then. We know that. But you might have had a very small amount in premium bonds. It only takes one pound to win a million, you know. Or one lottery ticket to get a big win. You don't need to be specific, just say you've had a lucky windfall, which you have."

Tony took a deep breath then blew it out through puffed cheeks.

"Looks like a decision made then," said Tony, holding out his hand to Sarah. "What do you think?"

She looked into his face and hesitated, then closed her eyes and sighed. "Yes." She opened her eyes and nodded decisively. "Yes."

The sound of a car horn tooting outside brought us back to reality.

"That will be your taxi." I moved to the window and gave the driver a wave.

Sarah stood up and picked up her handbag then we all walked through to the hall. Titus disappeared for a moment, as the rest of us hugged and said our goodbyes, then reappeared in the hall to shake hands with Tony and hand him the carrier bag containing the red outfit.

"Don't forget this," he said, then moved across to give Sarah a hug. They left, hurrying down the garden path and into the taxi, waving as it pulled away.

I locked the door and we moved together into the lounge and automatically started to gather up the glasses and plates.

"I think a cup of tea would go down well. What do you say?" I was already starting to load the dishwasher, but looked across at him with a grateful, "Yes please!" and Titus filled the kettle. We worked together, silently, for a few minutes, each wrapped in our own thoughts. When everything was tidy and the tea made, we sat at the kitchen table with our mugs.

"Well, back to normal life," I said. "No more excitement."

"We can still do the envelope drops," said Titus, "and something else may come up, you never know. We've not saved the world entirely you know. There will be something else."

I looked at him across the kitchen table.

"I wish I'd met you years ago," I said.

"I wish I'd met you, too. We'd have made a formidable team. We do make a formidable team." We smiled at each other.

"Mind you, if I'd met Trudy first, you wouldn't have stood a chance." He grinned at me and I chuckled.

"Do you think she really was recruited by MI5 or MI6 or something?" I wondered.

"Wouldn't be a bit surprised. She would have made a great Mata Hari. Do you want me to see what I can find out?"

I shook my head, smiling. "No. I think it's better as a mystery. It would be disappointing now to find out she wasn't."

We were quiet for a few more moments, sipping our tea.

"I'm really proud of James. What a turn around in him. I have apologised for misjudging him. But he was a bit of a scoundrel for a number of years. He never settled to anything. I suppose he's found his niche, his place in life. We all need to do that. It just takes some of us longer than others."

"And have you found yours yet, Lizzie?" Titus held my hand.

"Oh, I think so." I smiled. "I think I have, at last."

Chapter 19

The three Friday girls were buzzing with excitement as they shared the taxi home. They were already planning what date might be good to book their spa weekend and were thinking of something in about a month's time, but they would have to wait till they had checked if that suited Lizzie too. The taxi driver was watching them in the rear view mirror with an amused grin.

"You lot are worse than a fare of sixth formers on their way to a leaver's ball," he said. "You're chattering like a flock of starlings. What are you planning back there?"

"Oh we're just fixing up a girly weekend away." Trudy locked eyes with him in the mirror. Not bad looking. Slim, dark haired, about her age, looked like he might be into keeping fit. She moved slightly so she could see his hands on the steering wheel. No wedding ring.

"Did you draw the short straw then or do you always work a late shift?" she asked.

"I work any shift I can at the moment. A vindictive wife, soon to be ex-wife, took me for everything I had. Well, her and the divorce lawyer between them."

The three women made sympathetic noises as the taxi pulled up beside Pat's home.

The driver hopped out nimbly, giving Trudy the opportunity to sneakily take a better look at him as he opened the car door and held his hand out to Pat as she struggled out of the car. Mmm. Nice bum.

"Get your keys out love and I'll open the door for you," he said to Pat, then walked up the drive to the apartment block as she said her goodbyes. He hurried back down the path and handed the keys back to her then said, "Do you want to hold on to my arm love and I'll walk you to your door."

"I'm fine thank you." Pat was on her dignity and walked carefully away, turning to wave from the doorway.

"So who's next?" said the driver, turning round to look at his passengers as he fastened his seat belt.

"I'm just round the corner, so it's me next," said Sandra, and gave him directions. She exchanged taxi driving stories with him as they made their way through the quiet streets.

Ten minutes later they had dropped Sandra at her house and Trudy was left alone in the backseat. The atmosphere was charged as they drove the few miles to her apartment, but Trudy was not so badly smitten that she forgot her own rules. She might have given Geoff the impression she was flirty and 'up for it' but she had self respect. She wasn't about to rush headlong into a fling. They chatted in a stilted fashion but found out enough about each other to know that they were both interested in finding out more. When Trudy got out of the taxi and paid the fare the driver held out a company business card.

"If you need a taxi again anytime, this is our office number," he said. "And if I'm on duty you can ask for me." He turned the card over. "This is my name and my private number." He paused for a moment, still holding on to the card. "You can call me directly if you'd rather." He paused again. "Whether you need a taxi or not."

Trudy smiled and read the card wondering how many times a week he said that. Hopefully not many. "Thanks Pete." She took it and put it in her jacket pocket. "I'm Trudy. I might just do that." And she turned and entered the apartment block, aware that his eyes were watching her as she walked away from him.

Each of the women were undressed and ready for their beds within minutes of being in their homes. Sandra cleaned her teeth and was snuggled under the covers quickly, asleep almost before Trudy arrived home.

Trudy poured a glass of red wine from a bottle that she had opened the previous night, browsed the brochure for the spa weekend for a few minutes as she drank it, then undressed, popped to the bathroom and climbed into bed. The taxi business card was on her bedside table. She smiled to herself as she rested her head on the pillow. She might just take Pete up on that offer, and she turned over and put out the light.

Pat was the first to be dropped off but the last to think about going to sleep. Dressed in her cuddly dressing gown and fluffy slippers she made a hot chocolate then took out a bottle of brandy from the back of the kitchen cupboard and added a generous measure to the creamy mixture. She placed the mug on her kitchen table and went into her bedroom. Moving several pairs of boxed shoes from the bottom of her wardrobe she revealed the bare boards underneath. By pressing firmly at one end she caused the base to lift at the other. Pulling the base out she removed a laptop from the small space which was revealed. She took this back to the kitchen table, sat down and opened it up. After a few deft movements on the keyboard she sat back to sip her drink as she waited for a response.

It didn't take long before the screen changed colour and she quickly hit another key.

"Hello JD. Do you mind if we just use audio tonight? I'm not really dressed for the office and I'm not a pretty sight at this time of night."

"No problem, Ma'am. How have things gone?"

"Pretty much as predicted. No surprises. Everyone was delighted to get the gifts - a nice touch of yours, that. Tony and Sarah seemed a bit confused about the large amount but I think Titus and Lizzie will have convinced them. Trudy and Sandra don't know anything about that of course and that's how it should stay. I gather James was quite insistent that they should get a substantial amount. You are quite sure that he is as good as everyone thinks? It wouldn't be great if any of this was traceable."

"Absolutely, Ma'am, he's the best there is. Everyone who knows his work has no doubt about that. No sign of anyone being any the wiser about you, Ma'am?"

"No." Pat's tone was dismissive. "No danger there. They think I'm a jittery retiree who's nervous of her own shadow."

"Well you are officially retired, Ma'am, but we just don't seem to be able to manage without you. You keep coming up with more information and contacts. This latest caper has been very productive."

"Don't worry, JD, you will step into my shoes eventually." Pat wiggled her feet as she looked at the fluffy slippers she was wearing and imagined JD swapping his elegant, hand made brogues for something more relaxed.

"I must say, it's much easier to continue working now that everyone else is working from home too. When I first started doing it, I was considered quite an oddball."

JD made no comment. Pat suspected she was considered to be an oddball for many reasons and he didn't quite know how to respond without lying, being insensitive or even downright rude. She smiled. JD would never be openly rude. His public school education and years of training since then ensured that.

"How did it go from your end tonight?" she asked. "As well as we hoped?"

"No hitches that I am aware of Ma'am. Things are still ongoing but all good so far. This is going to be the biggest sting we have ever done."

"Well, keep me updated about progress."

"Yes, Ma'am and keep us aware of anything relevant from your end."

"I will JD. Enjoy the rest of your night."

"You too Ma'am. Goodnight."

Pat pressed a few more keys and her laptop screen went blank. She drained her mug, thought about pouring herself another brandy but decided against it and put the bottle away at the back of the cupboard. She took a few minutes to put the laptop away, replace the shoes, then pop to the bathroom but she was soon in bed, her eyes falling on the spa brochure on her bedside table as she tucked the duvet around her. She laid back and closed her eyes.

Yes, the spa weekend was a nice touch. She was looking forward to it.

The End

Acknowledgements

I'm grateful to Maggie Whitly for advice regarding refugees and asylum seekers and to my daughter for sharing relevant experiences. Any details which are not factually correct are due to my error or poetic licence.

Thanks to Liz Smith for telling me about the 'men in white hats' and other support and advice.

Peter and Sheila White, Lesley Hutchinson and Janet Peacock were helpful Beta Readers. Janet was also an excellent (and quick) copy editor. Any

remaining errors in grammar etc. are due to my tweaking of the story after she had checked it!

Finally, thanks as always to Rachel Weber. I could not publish anything without her expertise and artistic skills.

Jill Rodgers has also written:-

Rescue Ride

&

Max the Magnificent

Both books are chapter books for children aged approximately 6 - 9 years.

Available on Amazon

Jill Rodgers is a retired teacher with a great interest in promoting a love of reading in young children. She is married with two grown up children and five grandchildren. She and her husband love to spend time with family wherever possible, which is not always as often as they would like, as they live some distance away.

She has always enjoyed writing and initially wrote 'Rescue Ride' as a short story for her young children, after the family spent three weeks looking after a smallholding for some friends in a remote cottage in Yorkshire.

During Covid lockdown she revised and extended it for her grandchildren. Then, publishing the book, hoping it would be enjoyed by a wider audience, became important.

Learning about self publishing was a steep learning curve but eventually, with lots of help, her first book made it into print! 'Max the Magnificent' is a sequel to Rescue Ride, following the family as they move house with their dog Max.

Many of the events told in both stories are inspired by real life experiences and animals the family had over many years while living in a small Yorkshire village. 'I'm not holding the coats!' is her first novel for adults, written in response to a challenge by a member of the writers' group she attends. It has been another learning experience but a very enjoyable one and she looks forward to other challenges in the future.
July, 2023

Printed in Great Britain
by Amazon